THE CORRECT SADIST

The Memoirs of Angel Stern

by

TERENCE SELLERS

BLUE MOON BOOKS, INC.
NEW YORK, NEW YORK

The Correct Sadist
ISBN 1-56201-077-8
CIP data available from the Library of Congress

Manufactured in the United States of America
Published by Blue Moon Books, Inc.
61 Fourth Avenue
New York, NY 10003

Cover design by Steve Brower

Introduction

When I first read *The Correct Sadist* I was delighted and astonished. Here was a book that broke almost every literary convention yet which retained a perfect balance and consistency of style. What stuck in my mind then, and some two years on is still the strongest impression Terence Sellers' writing leaves with me, is the precision of her words, the way every phrase, letter, punctuation point is measured as though her very survival depended upon it. Nothing is thrown down without thought or purpose. Every sentence begs to be read and re-read. The tone, and it is very much Terence's voice we hear, is reminiscent of a decadent romanticism, a voice that speaks with a rare sense of honesty, and of a truth that resides within.

The Correct Sadist is without doubt an unusual book, and its publishing history is already extensive. Two editions have appeared in America, and translations have been published in Germany and France. In the text Terence takes the reader through the various psychic dramas that affect the Sadist and the Masochist, capturing both the harshness and poetic beauty of another reality. It quickly becomes very clear that we are dealing not with gratuitous acts of violence, but with an important part of human existence, that of the search for an emotional and psychological freedom, or wholeness. It has been said that there can be no beauty in violence — but there is a line where the violence acts as metaphor, especially when refined and controlled to the degree that it is within the Sadomasochistic drama. Indeed it is not the violence that is of importance but the dynamic of the relationship, the interchange between two beings. It is this area, which might well be defined as the search for Soul, that is at the heart of all Terence's writing. It is a search for an ultimate freedom from bondage through an examination of its most intimate and manifest intricacies.

It is a sad fact of modern life that conscious, stylised ritual is almost invariably confined to the most basic and undramatic arenas. Its purpose, of connecting ourselves to a wider and more encompassing consciousness has been subverted — in the main — to social norms, social methods of control. So ritual, other than in the socially defined areas of birth, marriage, death is largely devoid of its psychological import. And even in the principal rites of passage it is determined not by the needs of the participant but by a wider consensus of what is right, but which so often isn't on an individual level. In short such social rituals are no more than manifestations of social habit, devoid of the psychological elements that once caused them to arise. The result of this is that these social rituals not only ignore the true individuality of each of us, but at times are positively detrimental to our psychological well-being. The theme of Terence's work is the reclamation of that essential right to explore our own inner mind, our personal truth. And as is clear from the text this is a ritual process. From the early stages of verbal humiliation through to the final acts of apparent degradation the whole scenario is controlled and performed within well defined limits. Every act, every response is choreographed with extreme precision. Choice exists and is being exercised.

The immediate subject matter of the book is complemented by its inner content, the form of a ritual being after all only a surface manifestation of a deeper psychological dynamic. What interested me when I first read *The Correct Sadist*, and interests me now, is primarily that deeper level: the 'why?' What is it that drives the Mistress Angel Stern and her collaborators in sadomasochistic acts? That question bears no easy answer, yet it seems that the driving force must come from within, must be an integral part of the unconscious process of personal realisation. This process is most clearly seen in the first and last sections of the book where the Mistress Angel Stern examines her own mind, her own contradictions and motivations. It is this, be it in the specialised arena of Sadomasochism or in more commonplace areas of life, that affects all of us: is our freedom illusory or real?; are our actions helping or hindering our aims?; and from where do such ideas come? No book can answer these questions completely, but some — and *The Correct Sadist* falls within this category — help us to look at them, provide us with a new perspective that even for a moment may clear away the mist.

One further point should be made. The style of the sadomasochistic relationship is an odd one. It mirrors with a startling clarity the major aspect of societal control, that of command and service. This pervades all, or nearly all, human activity, most noticeably in the public arena where each of us takes on, quite often unwittingly, a position of Higher or Lower within a hierarchical structure. We command here, but serve there. This is clearest in the broadly termed and meticulously stratified military services, but it exists equally within all other spheres of human relationship, in the choices we make and the results of those choices on those around us. Truly the pervasiveness of the game is intense. Choices are pre-conditioned by what others say is reasonable for someone in our circumstance, and modified by our personal ego, our imperfect vision of who we are. Is this really choice at all?

The Sadist and the Masochist address these limitations of choice, as Terence Sellers shows, in a direct fashion. They put aside the 'reasonable' and for a moment in time create a ritual space in which the rules are written afresh. They may appear meaningless or absurd outside the special context, but within they are all, and allow both participants an equal right to express some part of themself that is denied expression elsewhere. What is clear is that by 'acting out' the participants create a highly charged and highly personal alter-identity, that is neither themselves nor not-themselves. This alter-identity is a part of them and is in fact the Dominant within the SM scenario. The day-to-day persona vanishes for the moment both for the individual taking on the role of, or acting as, Superior, and for the one who acts as Masochist. It is a direct communion between two 'Others'. And in a sense it is also an act of psychic hygiene that creates the space in which a true understanding of who we are can materialise. This we see in the Mistress Angel Stern's discussion of her own psychic health, her own analysis of why she acts so, and where it leads.

Terence's remarkable text not only talks of this relationship between 'Others', but manifests it within the chosen structure of the novel. The harsh, almost unreal, relentlessness of the scenes displays exactly the strangeness of the relationship, the very 'otherness' of it. What we have is far removed from what we usually perceive as human dialogue and exchange. Instead two strangers live out a perfect enclosed drama (dream) without any intrusion. It is a private, hermetic world. Terence Sellers shows that world as it is. A world where nothing is quite what it seems, where the boundary between dreams and reality flickers momentarily out of focus and allows a new perspective to take form.

Words
Temple Press Limited
Brighton, England. 23/11/89

. . . the entire morality of improvement, the Christian included, has been a misunderstanding . . . To have to combat one's instincts — that is the formula for decadence: as long as life is ascending, happiness and instinct are one.

Friedrich Nietzsche,
Twilight of the Idols

Foreword

I desire no one to follow me along this path where by flaunting my choice to behave evilly I hoped to provoke the wrath of the Authority. Yet in judging and punishing others as I failed to judge and punish myself I myself created the Authority as the outside witness my cowardice required.

I desire in the wake of this revealment to prepare a sterile ground where now flourishes a pestilent growth. I hope to succeed so well that the techniques of degradation herein described will poison the reader with the consciousness of their ubiquity; and may the future reader be so free as to regard them as pitiable and quaint! So do I invoke my obsolescence, but I leave these traces behind. Through this murk did I advance, faint clues to the correctness of my will clearing the haze, though rarely, with a devastating clarity.

1

Bad Blood

I have always considered myself unknown to others. When anyone attempted to pierce my guardian shell, I never doubted they would soon give up under the strain of so futile and unrewarding a project. Yet I did await the day when I could reveal to someone my soul, that would then burst out so brilliantly white it would annihilate us all . . .

All the so-called terrors of solitude console me. The resonant silence of the evening's end, as the stars come into their own is a pleasure I cannot share with anyone — though some do seem sensitive enough. I often awake alone, with the echo of an uncertain sound from the house below fading in my ears . . . I leap from the bed directly and rush to meet the intruders. Perhaps once a week I have such an adventure. But no one is ever there.

One evening when I was ten I embraced the form of the full white moon as my only 'husband'. I stretched out on my bed under its sickly light and submitted to a weird alertness. The room fell away and I strained towards the open window. The real world was not of blue walls, books in bookcases, not my sister sleeping in the next bed, not school and my lessons done for tomorrow — but something awful, and tense; it was a struggle and the presence of death. The climax of this tremulous dislocation was the palpable knowledge that I was not my body even if I should try to be. I then realized my bed as the wide end of a great wedge whose blade was buried in the centre of the earth — and from my spine fell a plumb line to this single point.

At seventeen I lived in the arid red landscape of New Mexico whose dry hostility suggested the surface of the moon. Returning from some amusement one night, I crossed a brushy plain and realized too late I had walked directly into a lunar communion, the submission of that charred land to the violent spew of full moon-light. I panicked and walked faster, and had the misfortune to look down at my feet. Between my raised foot and the ground gaped a vast space. My foot drifted down and hit with a sickening vertigo, my leg turned to amoeba and I fell — and in the luxury of that fall I wished there was no earth to receive me. Yet once safely prone I clung to a little stubble of brush and suffered that familiar moon-wash of illogic, of confusion, of *suspension* in every pore. Terror ebbed away and I was not I was a multitude of beings, and so released . . .

Even though I am well-armoured against your interest and violations, never do I suffer slightly any influence from without. I absorb you readily, immediately do I become your subject. Yet I never let you see this. I once thought this was symptomatic of my desire to be of a heart sublime and devoted beyond all others, but were I indifferent or obsessed all contacts were intimate and excruciant. For once you are admitted, in the effort I make to comprehend your alien soul, I revoke my right to solitude and thus am utterly lost to myself.

In the naive enthusiasm of a new companionship (it always holds the promise of an ideal realized!) I would not notice my new vacancy. I felt far from empty for I was inhabited by them. My chosen one's gestures, grimaces, turns of phrase and even their laugh soon replaced my own. It took but one disharmony for the inevitable to occur. With a spasm of self-disgust I knew the innecessity of the chosen one, and so withdrew proudly, suppressing my real sorrow . . . But I was unknown to them throughout, and the scourge that is my true and better self rallied against what I could now perceive as their parasitism. Ruthlessly did I expel every drop of their influence from my pores, and by this purging believed I destroyed every quality I had possessed in common with their inferior person.

Why did I continue to seek them out, when my virulent idealism doomed the contact?

Like some exotic monster I rarely emerged from the green darkness of the ocean floor, where my frail phosphorescence lit the way. These light and fluent creatures, who fled easily through watery latitudes to surface and air I envied; I wondered at their careless trust in a foreign light. I surface slowly into their bright and confused stream to find they care nothing about my icy home below. They know only that to follow me would be their death as slowly the terrible pressure crushed their bodies. Enough that they are well-amused by my lurid colouring and profusion of antennae.

As a child I did not consider myself a child. At birthday parties I wheedled my way into the room where the adults sat drinking, and I danced and amused them and pretended to understand everything they said. No amount of prodding could induce me to return to the noisy games, and if I was taken forcibly into the children's company, with disapproval and scolding as though I were being punished, they in turn would reject me, and make me the butt of their play.

I used to lie to myself concerning my parentage and true home. Lied? No, I had not the faintest doubt that my parents were not my real ones. As an infant I had been abandoned by the royal pair who had conceived me. It was all because of the war. I recalled the basket that I had been found in: of dark golden straw decorated with green paint and swathed in a gauzy protective canopy. A bouquet of violets were tucked in at the foot of the snow-white coverlet. I often dwelt upon the names of the gems: diamond, ruby, emerald, sapphire, for these were the playthings of my lost childhood. By some awful fluke my true parents had never rediscovered me, and so was I doomed to live out the balance of my early years miserably, within the narrow, institutional grey walls of a one-bedroom apartment. Mansion, canopy, chandelier, balustrade — I recited these words as an immigrant strives to keep his homeland tongue alive. I considered my adoptive parents malicious in their design to keep me from my proper station in life and felt few qualms in being completely disobedient. Crystal, throne, angel, salon — these were the words of my proper language.

Thus did I reluctantly develop within a childhood fraught with hardship and humiliation. Perhaps it was no worse than any childhood but to a vagrant princess it was a cruel purgatory. My one consolation was school, where I assumed my natural predominance. Insufferably good at my lessons, a toady to my teachers, my classmates loathed me. I detested them as a nest of snakes. I made my closest friend in a girl to whom I had to concede first place from time to time. In that way I leached of its odiousness her occasional triumph over me.

I took as a mark of distinction the scornful treatment, jibes and petty snubs I received as a consequence of my hauteur. If my blueblood was not recognized the soul of the beholder was in affliction, not I. This belief in my innate aristocracy and imminent assumption into the aery, ineluctable regions of a spiritual royalty was my solitary and inviolable experience of conviction.

The stories of the lives of the saints never failed to seduce me. Morbidly was I attracted to those that recounted the most horrifying physical trials, the sacrificial punishments endured for the glory of God. The life of an ascetic hermit in the desert I envied, it seemed the most perfect of lives. About these hermits I was extremely curious, but upon their destitution and exalted communion with God the nuns would not remark. Instead of revealing to me the reason behind this behaviour, they turned my eyes towards the banal saints, who plodded in their gardens and taught little children. I was left to my own devisings, and designed to emulate the holy men's sublime excesses. I believed it was within my power to take up such a life, but the nun to whom I revealed this vocation quickly discouraged me. She falsified a schedule of the arduousness of achieving that 'position': insisted that I would have to enter a cloistered convent; that it took years and years to learn how to meditate; that the Vatican now disapproved of people 'avoiding their duties in the world, and using prayer as an escape'.

I considered a hair-shirt. I practised sleeping on the floor, half-way through the night I relented and stole a pillow from the bed . . . I settled for buckling my belt too tightly and wearing old shoes. Over and over I read the lives of my favourites — St. Theresa in particular — and gratified myself through evoking their trials. Their torments and ecstasies I rapturously envisioned as other adolescents no doubt call up the phantom arms of film-stars. I withdrew from the profane world, 'mere material existence', but grew frustrated and languid under the influence of my simulations. The pristine impact of a vision was not forthcoming; Theresa transfigured by a spasm was simpler than I . . .

I cannot now recall the name of the saint who washed the feet of lepers, who as proof of her humility before the most afflicted of God's creatures drank the dirty bath-water. The peril of this did not satisfy, no — she would catch in her throat a loosened scab from one of their incurable sores, swallowing it with thanks, as no different from the Eucharistic Body of Christ Himself. This accomplishment I admired and dwelt upon. I could not comprehend why the Church did not find glory in these acts. Whatever God had responded to these ecstatic submissions had fallen under suspicion.

Gradually the Church whose rituals I had ardently observed and whose saints I emulated came to disappoint me. I began to know the back of the nun's hand as my waxing bad faith sloughed off the restraint of fear. Their displeasure made me cynical as I dispiritedly marked in them a strange repressed rage that focused too avidly upon the palest disobedience.

The terms of my exile grew clearer as my enervate, lonely adolescence dragged on. I asked myself with debilitating frequency: how much longer must I remain on the outside, cut off from the state of grace? The power of the confessional was a confidence trick — there was no-one to confide in, certain stains would never fade. A more potent exorcist I required to relieve the brand of strangeness that was upon me. Thus was I compelled to embrace my estrangement, and passionately; beneath its cold triumphant form my moral sense ceased to function.

Due no doubt to my increasing inhumanity my family expelled me from my home as soon as I was of age. A naive and arrogant confidence in the power of my intellectual ability assured me this was to my taste, for whatever I wanted I could have by the mere willing. I rapidly discovered that these cerebral virtues were considered just so much decoration by the Philistine. I had no practical resources upon which to draw, and soon I decided to reconcile myself with the strangers who were my family. But such hostility had I provoked in them it is no exaggeration to say they wished me dead, or mad. My letters to them returned unopened.

The demeaning job I was reduced to taking was not the worst of it, but that the world had only that to offer me I took as a personal insult. My assumption into the company of the Elect was still years away, and I sensed this and so conferred upon myself a tragic air. The money I earned paid for the animal's keep: food and shelter, and nothing else.

Under the influence of the meagre meals, the cheap clothes I scavenged, the derelict apartment I barricaded myself within, my nerves' strength declined. I became convinced that luxury held in its symbols the spiritual food for which I starved. To recall that the hermit suffered worse privations failed to console me; for my temperament was in truth sensuous, worldly and proud. Poverty gave the lie to my power and obscured the nobility I was destined for. There were forces abroad bent on my destruction; jealous ones, lusting after my inheritance. They rejoiced to see my demoralization, and against this vast organization of evil I was a weak and solitary dreamer.

I renewed my convictions; I shut myself away and devoted all my thoughts and acts to regaining contact with the kingdom of the Elect. From my readings in books of magic ritual, in the histories of foundling empires won by blood, in the brain-sick songs of Baudelaire I came to suspect it was incorrect to sit and wait for the crown to descend from the skies. I had to steal it back, from those who kept it from me. What right had they? Through my own devising I would enter the company of the Elect. Under the spell of this moral imperative I floundered, irritated past breathing, frustrated and sickened by my absolute ignorance of method.

It was in this unbalanced and aspiring mental state that I commenced to read a most malignant writer, but one who unflinchingly proclaimed a virtuosity in the use of power. An aristocrat by birth, he was not satisfied by the conventional ascendance he held; his temperament prompted him to delve more deeply into the arts of manipulation, of the victorious assault. This philosophy sounded a deep and sonorous knell within me; it freed me, and so condemned me to destroy all I had held sacred — without sentimental retractions. Nor did this resonance fade over several months; it became my daily work to obey the imperative to overcome myself. This appeal to my courage became absolute, and I recognized attack *as the key*. The repeated drain of their insinuations demanded it of me; so did I tap into my death-dealing instinct.

Much of what I found embedded in his writings was a vicious and empty power, wholly temporal and polluted by commonplace sexual lust. But the efficacy of his methods, the orderliness of his realm, and the invigorating constant of the attainment of his desires I could not deny. If my end was not the same as his could I not, still, use his means?

Once the weights and measures of Authority were in my hand I would do with them as I pleased. The means would not determine the end! In the practice of certain physical manipulations, simple and subtle, ritualized and clear; by incorporating into my vocabulary the words and phrases I deemed intrinsic to an aristocracy of mind; by assuming the conviction that whatsoever I thought, spoke or did was correct, I would prepare the ground for my future dominion, develop in myself the shell of Authority, and so become more like and thereby worthy of the Elect to whose company I aspired.

Thus I cultivated my sadism; I styled myself a Lucifer to attract the attention of God. It was only logical. His displeasure and punishment was preferable to the stagnant limbo where I now formlessly crept.

Criminal was this impulse, and I followed it, devoting myself to the practice of sadism as essential to my development. What was moral law to me? I recognized it as propaganda to weaken smaller minds and open them to my pincers. I needed at last obey nothing but my own conviction of grandeur.

Thus I entered into the sphere of the professional sadist. The orderliness of the business transaction seemed to excise moral considerations from my acts, and rewarded me besides with money enough to buy the luxuries I required. I was provided with a steady, willing stream of victims I could experiment upon anyway I liked. The men were forced to present themselves as johns, that is, pathetic beggars who had to pay to satisfy their perverted desires. I employed the persona of the prostitute as a further instrument of their degradation. The masochist has little physical contact with his 'Mistress' but an abusive one, precluding all acts of intercourse, kisses, all fond caresses. This was entirely agreeable as I held the sexual act, particularly between man and woman, to be one of the more loathesome pastimes of humanity.

When I first embarked upon this vocation I rejoiced in my freedom to indulge in a psychic orgy of narcissism and violence, without there being any question of a victim's revenge. My first act, when presented with a masochist, was to put him in bondage so he could not escape me. As soon as I realized he was helpless, I relaxed in a very peculiar way. My back straightened and my head poised floatingly upon my neck. My arms and legs moved slowly and with a dreamlike precision that seemed hydraulic; my torso was subject to hallucinations of being a kind of metallic pivot, or hinge. These sensations that came on upon the masochist's forced submission were symptoms of my increasing conviction of the impersonality of my will, and so of my invulnerability. The exaltation in controlling every word and act, and in time every thought of another intoxicated me; and so evolved an addiction.

After the masochist's bondage began a vituperative monologue. The victim was first impressed with his physical repulsiveness, that this was evidence of his lowness of character. In this way he was forced to accept the idea of his essential bondage to a more or less hideous physical shell. The monologue then evolved along the lines of the victim's particular theme: that he was a bad child, or a dog, or that he was a sinner, that he merited castration, or that he was a sewer. The variations were numerous, but always he was a base creature. The finale of my diatribe was a sort of anthem I developed over the years, that I felt epitomized for the victim his place in life: that he was essentially a degenerate, a subhuman, and temperamentally incapable of rising above the muck where he gladly wallowed. Insults flooded out of me with all the ease of inspiration, the most vile and twisted ideas.

I occasionally looked on in amazement at the venomous force that came from her. But I told myself she was the medium for this force, and not the force itself. I thrilled to use myself as the field for the strenuous battle of sadist contra masochist. I saw the operation of these opposing forces everywhere, and elicited it from every situation. In time, the effect of my power was no longer confined to the conscious few who admitted to their sexual masochism. I came to be an inspiration to many to practise cruelty in a methodical fashion.

But one evening the intervention of this observant self who for so long had witnessed the derangements 'she' encouraged, the perversions 'she' fostered and that 'she' then miraculously cured, now severely recalled me to the original task I had set myself; now what was the true purpose of my sadism?

So remote had this end become, so involved was I with the intricate methods of control for the pleasure of control, she could say without flinching: No purpose! There is no meaning, what are you, a sophomore? Life is ugly, and useless! . . . I had not quite forgotten my royal destiny, but I no longer worried about it. I expected nothing from the Elect, though I felt sure of prison. I found some pleasure, too, in the prospect of a cell. At last, like the hermits! I thought some about repentance, I backslid in a hundred other tiny ways, back to the vigilance of the nuns, I felt I was being watched as I tortured and abused my victims . . . many of whom were very attached to me and smiled radiantly as I spat in their faces.

By degrees all the influence I had acquired slipped away; I saw I controlled only neurotic babies who deludedly adored me; and it was not even myself they adored but an abstraction. I could not enforce my own ideas of obedience, for I was required to act as an ambassador for some greater power who unfailingly intruded itself and who by right exacted this obedience. That I too was at its disposal repelled me unspeakably, and incited me to more repulsive indulgences. To those of healthy robust character my superiority was a species of psychosis.

Between the tantrums in the torture chamber and the hauteur I affected in society an impassable abyss widened. Within it I was persecuted by an obscure and hateful Authority. My indulgence in certain forms of behaviour — foul language, complaining, demands to be admired and catered to, relentless criticizing — had rendered me intolerant of a non-submissive personality. A world empty of the slavish soul would herald my extinction. Any discipline I had formerly possessed dissipated under the brutal ardour of my narcissism.

I could simulate self-control when in the presence of others, as the persona of the dominatrix demanded. But when alone as I found myself increasingly I did not bother to dissimulate. I no longer gazed at her violence astonished, nor did I warn or scold her. I attacked myself, tore at my heart with a ravenousness I could term *appetite*. I had an appetite for killing myself, and while crying or confessing brought some relief, more often did this hysterical *victim's* outburst degenerate into a masochistic display. Under the strain of the rule of the sadist this animal part of me, uncontrollable, grew wilder and wilder. It seemed to the sadist there was but one recourse contra the repeated outbreaks of self-pity, of longing for love, and that was to kill herself and 'til she did she was a worthless coward.

It was only proper that she kill herself now that she had discovered that she was one of the inferior specimens. If she truly believed in the rule of the Elect she would sacrifice herself to this ideal, not dribble on pretending to be alive.

But I was the correct sadist, and she was me; there was no distinction between us. She was my creation, and now all that was real . . . yet unreal too as I saw myself her slave. For she did hold in her hands the techniques to gain power, and naturally she first wielded them over me. As I considered this bondage I observed a certain void had been fashioned in my heart by her presence, a void like a tiny, insistent maelstrom. It ate at the weak, it fed upon affliction, it possessed an appetite for carrion that would not be sated. So I did nothing to dissuade my slaves from their submission, for when I tormented them I no longer suffered from self-hatred.

Then I could elicit the obsessive notion that it was my right to receive their sickly veneration. I knew a morbid satisfaction in clinging to the idea that I possessed a special sensibility that penetrated and loved the secretive, the dark side of the moon I knew as my rightful province. As well I could not avoid remarking a real, preponderant slavishness in humanity, that had neither conception nor desire to conceive of a spiritual privilege. These persons were all particularly subject to a sadistic influence and it was incumbent upon me to rule them. For as I am created in the image of Cruelty, so they realize their victim nature in grovelling before me. I become the reason for their vacancy, for their lack of control. You see I am no common vampire.

Why I came to the decision to describe in these pages the methods of controlling the tedious syndrome that is masochism is complex: primarily I wished to remember what I had learned. I considered very little an audience as I wrote. I hoped to be able to come to the end of the subject, and have done with sadomasochism altogether. For brief periods I believed these methods, applied rigorously, would cure masochism. But there is no cure, only the alleviation of pressure. The idea that inferiority could be a delusion does not impress the masochist. For to lose control in the presence of a Greater is their religious pleasure. The door is opened gladly to a mortal wound, and romantically named nemesis. Against it one may wage an elaborate war, with rites of mortification, chases, attacks, battle-losses and crownings.

I may demonstrate again and again the use of the lock upon this door, but in my participation in the chronic breaking-in I myself go numb to the possibility of sealing the door.

That indeterminate sound from the house below: it's *her*, unlatching the door to take a midnight stroll. She cannot stay put at night, the air is too thrilling . . .

I must maintain the integrity of my criminality, impossible now to retrace my steps. A sentimental idea! Let them lock me out all night. I will not repent, intolerable constriction, I have done more than ten persons in their lifetimes could pay for. I wonder often who will come to revenge themselves upon me . . . who will claim my head? To release me from myself and return me to my true home? I can say with conviction I have made formidable enemies throughout my career. But I will stay deep in the entrails of the early hour where I remain unchallenged . . . for they are of the established strength and they are very well organized. They would count it a great success to exterminate me. I fly in the face of their threats, their ranting, and I am not, I tell you, even mildly irritated by these puny restraints. For I cannot be destroyed.

2
The Leeching

Basic Etiquette for the Slave

These ground-rules must be insisted upon by the Superior and obeyed from the start or else the slave is to be rejected as unfit material for manipulation.

One: *He will at all times address the Superior as 'Mistress' or 'Master'. You may require him to use a variation on this title such as 'Divine Queen Goddess', 'Father Confessor', 'Supreme Being', as you like. He may not use the possessive pronoun, i.e., he may not say 'My Mistress' as he is the one owned.*

Two: *He may never present himself at full height but remains below the waist or knees of the Superior on his knees or belly. Enjoin him to keep his little paws to himself, at his sides or behind him. No other pose is acceptable.*

Three: *He may open his mouth only to answer direct questions, fetch, or receive dispensations. If he absolutely will irritate the Superior's ears he must ask permission to speak, which is in itself an act of disobedience.*

Four: *The slave ought to be compelled to appear in some form of humiliation-wear you have chosen. Standard humiliation-wear is the underwear of the opposite sex and will do until you designate a special role for him such as hooker, or baby, when he will be dressed accordingly.*

Five: *If he is employed as maid, try to relieve yourself of the bother of constantly ordering his inept person about by training him to anticipate your wishes. He will of course be punished for assuming too much, for trying to make his uselessness indispensable.*

Six: *Impress the slave that he ought to submit gratefully to your orders, whims and cruelties, that an incredibly fortunate intervention of fate has bestowed upon his pathetic life a purpose he would never have realized by himself. That the Superior considers him material amenable to manipulation ought to be a source of joy, for most slaves are so essentially worthless it is a waste of time trying to make anything of them.*

Seven: *Hammer it into his pea-brain that he has no will but to do as the*

Superior commands him to do. The Superior may delegate this authority to another whom he must obey as unconditionally as he would the beloved Superior in person. For the Superior knows best what the slavish soul needs, and unless he puts his full trust in her influence he will remain a craven dog without a home.

Preparation of the Slave

The Superior finds the body of the slave more or less repulsive until it has been hygienically prepared to come into contact with her. A thorough cleansing, inside and out, the shaving of at least the pubic region, and bondage are the three preliminaries for the imposition of servitude.

While some may argue that the enema's best result is in its weakening effect — so the slave is rendered agreeably limp — this is secondary to the psychological debilitation produced by the enema. If administered properly, the slave's body is not only freed of all dead matter but is so purified he will experience a sense of release from a previous cycle. This leaves him open and fresh to your influence. The passivity induced by the enema is not so much that of the weak, but of the new-born. Unquestionably it is the best way to render the nervous novice amenable.

Some may prefer to administer a douche of ice-cold water to induce cramping. This effect may be increased by adding liquid detergent to the water. Drano is not recommended, though it is certainly appropriate. Another variation is to fill the bag with the 'golden shower', thereby impressing upon the slave the excrement of the Superior is so pure it may be used to clean him. Wine may be added to the water to produce instant drunkenness. None of these are to my taste — especially the last as it deadens the nerves.

The most healthful method is to use one or two quarts of very hot water without additives, and require the slave to lie on his left side and rub his stomach from right to left as the enema flows into him so that the water moves through his entire colon. A repetition of this process is recommended. "What should you do to clean out that Great Sewer Pipe, filling nearly or quite half your intestinal cavity, possibly so distended as to be thick through as your arm, choked, encrusted, and so packed full of hardened filth and foulness that its exhalations permeate your entire system, rendering your perspiration and your breath so foul it is plainly perceptible to others — how would you proceed to clean it out? Why flush it out, of course, you stupid!"* This vivid description of the horrors of the blocked gastro-intestinal tract is useful to corporate into your punishment dialogue with the slave. The positive and therapeutic effects of this hygienic ritual are quite punishing enough without more victimizing elaborations than the simple truth.

Make certain the slave eliminates all of the douche before he is thrown back out into the gutter from whence he came. A brief jogging session or five minutes of go-go dancing before fifteen minutes in the bathroom will suffice in this. The slave must be punished for offending odours that may reach the Superior's nostrils, though he is not told why he is being punished, lest he derive a nasty rebellious satisfaction from his misbehaviour.

The slave ought then to be given a cold bath, letting him soak for about half an hour in a solution of disinfectant and oil. He is thus rendered germ-free and malleable.

The Superior then has her assistant or the slave himself shave whatever area she wishes made particularly vulnerable. Any hairs left behind will be pulled out or burned off.

There is some disagreement on whether one's dominance is better complemented by a naked slave, or one dressed in a humiliating costume. The costume must be well-suited to the particular masochism of the slave, otherwise it will impress him as a piece of stupidity and incite him to rebellion. Do not dress your 'pig' in a school-boy's outfit; snap on his ears and insert his tail and he will graciously submit. When in doubt, leave him naked. A pair of ruffled panties does have a universally degrading appeal. As well it saves the Superior from the mild disgust suffered at the sight of the slave's genitals. For masochistic

**The Hindu Yogi Practical Water Cure* by Yogi Ramacharaka, Yogi Publication Society, 1937.

women a soiled pair of men's jockey shorts serves the same purpose. The full-blown fetish for cross-dressing and its ambiguities will be discussed further on.

The slave is now prepared for bondage.

Bondage

Bondage is a creative activity; some may have a special knack for it, while the rest may do well to master a few simple techniques they may elaborate upon as they gain more experience.

In this modern age there are available all types of bondage furniture from mail-order houses. The use of these devices is self-evident, based as they are in large upon Puritan stocks and whipping posts, medieval racks and cages. For those fortunate enough to possess them, they make up in efficiency and dramatic appeal what they lose in creativity. One can just as well practise restraining a victim on such commonplace objects as beds, sofas, over chairs or toilets, across doorways, etc.

Prior to any torture, spanking or whipping it is a good idea to restrain the subject, unless he is exceedingly submissive. But no matter how masochistic they are, under the torturing hand there will always be resistance. Indeed to resist is half the pleasure. But one must reduce to a minimum the amount of thrashing about for tortures to be effected with precision and without accident.

The use of nylon or cotton rope, fine copper chain or a steel chain and shackle, handcuffs or thumb-cuffs, specially fashioned leather or rubber restraints is entirely up to the sensuality of the Superior. As well, some slaves will not feel as restrained in chain as they would in rope, whose submissiveness cannot fully unfurl unless they be strung up with a certain material in a particular position. A dull steel shackle and chain is rather comic and theatrical, and good for light bondage; a dirty, greasy hemp rope evokes a more nasty, butch atmosphere. Some Mistresses need only use their stockings to restrain their slaves. Style may be myriad, but end is single.

The Superior may have a few positions specifically to his or her taste as most humiliating, but the torture to be inflicted usually dictates the form. For example, in sodomization the buttocks ought to be spread very wide and raised for an unrelenting penetration. The knees brought back towards the ears and secured is best for this. For virgins, leave the subject face down with a reasonable spread (the sight of the dildo or manhood is always unnerving). Tortures will require the maximum restraint. The hands and feet tied together hog-style behind the back, coupled with suspension relieves the subject of any fear of the Superior's slipping up with the razor blade, or what have you.

The point of bondage is to induce the sensation of helplessness essential to submission. The slave may consider himself a very passive individual, but he has not felt it upon his body, imposed from without by another. The psychodrama of finding himself in bondage palpably mirrors his profound conviction of inferiority, and creates in the slave, when he is released, a kind of rebound of the will that is highly beneficial. It occurs that any feeling or idea of entrapment, oppression, limitation and the like no longer sorely aggravates the slave/subject, after the crude physical restraint of bondage. Hence the use of solitary confinement as a discipline for violent prisoners; once out of the horror of total confinement, confinement to one building does not seem so desolate. The judgement of the Superior ought carefully to weigh the relationship between the extent of the psychological 'bind', and the style of bondage to be used, as well as the length of time the slave is left in bondage. Too severe, or too mild a bondage will fail to assuage the inferior feelings of the slave, causing him to question your authority and turn defensive.

Now and then one meets up with a slave who whines, "I'm not into bondage." They are either very well-trained, or merely afraid. The Master or Mistress will quickly discern which of the two is the case. For example, if the slave does not realize his place is on his knees or belly, below the knees of the Superior, he is ill-trained. If the slave uses his hands without being told to, touching himself or the Superior without permission; if he talks back or behaves in an insolent manner; if he constantly whines and demands the Superior spank him or torture him this way or that; if he will not take the Superior's word as law and manifests a will of his own; all such infractions will be met with a bondage punishment. As well, it is highly agreeable to the delicate nervous system of the Superior that the slave is left alone in bondage for him to brood over his predicament and realize he has no choice.

There are slaves for whom bondage alone is sufficient to produce the maximum pleasure. This claustrophilia springs from the desire to be possessed by the Superior — to be kept secure, to be protected, to be held captive. For example, there is the 'cocoon'. The slave is first gagged, hands and feet tied together not very tightly with rope. He is then wound up in a sheet of cotton, or a special rubber or leather sheet, the cocoon secured by yards of rope or chains, so you are left with a very neat bundle. A part to be punished, such as the genitals or buttocks, may be left free as part of a fantasy of exposure and abandonment (see dialogue). Slaves who favour this 'mummification' discipline also enjoy being locked away for hours in a closet or cage. Variations on the theme include wrapping the face of the slave in a fetish item under the bondage; requiring he not soil himself within his package lest he be punished; using the 'package' as furniture, mattress or a chair or table. Simple rough treatment like dragging, kicking and knocking about may follow; to inflict a severe punishment over the bondage precludes marking the body, an advantage often desired. All are in harmony with the tastes of the bondage addict. As well it may be the very last word in sadistic pleasure for the Superior, as she can let go completely with all the physical abuse she is capable of without really damaging the slave, enclosed as he is in his ecstatic cocoon.

Dialogue between Prison Warden and Prisoner

The Mistress is the Prison Warden; she may wear some sort of military regalia. The slave is in rags or naked, and in completely immobilizing bondage in a closet/cell.

Mistress: *You know why you are here.*

Slave: *Yes, Warden.*

Warden: *You are going to be here, with us, for the next twenty years, because of your crimes.*

Prisoner: *Let me go! Let me free! (Struggles against his chains.) You can't do this! I want to go out on the yard with the rest of the guys!*

Warden: *And get raped again?*

Prisoner: *Well . . . anything's better than being in solitary confinement!*

Warden: *You prisoners don't understand that everything we do for you is good for you. If I took you out of here you would be raped repeatedly until you were killed, you're such a tender little piece of chicken.*

Prisoner: *Do you think so?*

Warden: *Myself . . . and others.*

Prisoner: *Will you come and visit me often?*

Warden: *I come and visit all my little boys in solitary.*

Prisoner: *But how long do I have to stay here?*

Warden: *(Patting his head.) Until you grow up and are more of a man and can protect yourself against the big bullies.*

Prisoner: *But what if they try to break in here?*

Warden: *The guards will be here to protect you.*

Prisoner: *Are they all as beautiful as you?*

Warden: *Yes.*

Prisoner: *(Struggling and writhing.) Oh . . . I don't know what's worse. Being the butt-boy of all the macho men in the prison, or being at your mercy.*

Warden: *Calm down, calm down, there's nothing you can do about it. We've made the decision for you. You're going to be here for a long time, and we'll see to it that you are not let out of your cell.*

Prisoner: *I feel like I'm going to be here forever . . . Are you going to keep me here forever . . .? Please keep me . . . I'll do work for you.*

Warden: *Yes, the guards and I make all the prisoners in solitary work very hard for us.*

Prisoner: *What do you make us do?*

Warden: *You have to cater to our every need . . . We check you all out for talent and give you jobs according to your abilities.*

Prisoner: *Wipe your feet on me . . . use me as a toilet . . .*

Warden: *We'll decide on it.*

Slave begins a glazed recital of all the degrading things he will be forced to do. Mistress agrees or disagrees with his fantasies according to her whim. Slave is convulsively rubbing himself against his bindings, the bars of the cage, the floor, etc.

Prisoner: *You bitch . . . let me out.*

Warden: *You are a menace to society and a degenerate and you can never leave in your whole life. The jury lied to you. You are in for life.*

Prisoner: *I don't want to be controlled by you . . . Force me to service the other men . . .*

Warden: *Never.*

Slave suffers his orgasm at this refusal to let him indulge his masochistic homosexuality.

Corporal Punishment — Whipping and Spanking

Ordinarily, corporal punishment is meted out to a child who disobeys the wishes of his parents. These wishes are at best not whimsical, but developed as essential to the well-being of the child. Ideally the child will associate destructive forms of behaviour with pain, which acts as a deterrent against the repetition of the forbidden act. In this way does the child learn to discipline *himself.*

However, when a warning has been attached to a destructive act, it may occur that the act is invested with the mysterious aura of a taboo that serves as an incitement to again indulge the act. If the child's private pleasure, or his sexual curiosity towards other children is neither restrained by his own self-discipline, nor dissuaded by the prospect of punishment, the child grows attached to his rule-breaking and will accept as part of his pleasure the certainty of punishment.

The older the child becomes, the more cunning he is in his avoidance of the punishment for his pleasure. He realizes that punishments are not instantly precipitated from the act — that one must be caught. He may presume that nothing will happen to him if he is never caught. This naive immorality chooses to ignore the long-term effects of heavy boozing; does not concern itself with the impairment done to his sexual health through chronic masturbation. He does not care to understand that the acts are a form of self-inflicted punishment — since they at present give so much pleasure. The masochistic temperament adamantly refuses to recognize the logical outcome of a vicious indulgence — and within the limbo, between the act and its consequences, the masochist is granted the time to indulge his exciting self-destruction. As well within this hiatus there flourishes the vague and hydra-headed guilt, that first the parental authority, and later the Superior holds over his head.

How readily is guilt removed, for the child, by the swift and timely intervention of a paddling on the rear. Crime, and the authority's displeasure with the crime are experienced as two inseparable, complementary dynamics. As he grows older and the consequences of his behaviour are less immediately realized, the more acutely does he suffer from guilt. Even as the consequences are realized, the guilt is still intense, for the masochist is often incapable of blaming and punishing himself for his bad behaviour. He fails at self-retribution and longs for the punishments imposed by authority — jails, hospitals, legal action, divorces. For these punishments from without alleviate his guilt and so free him to again indulge his vice — at least, until the guilt builds up again.

So does the masochist make a ritual, an endless orgy of his self-indulgence and guilt. He believes in his guilt in a way that he cannot believe in his ability to reform. Pressure is temporarily relieved by punishment, but the masochist does not dare truly repent — to become the person for whom such acts are impossible — for all his pleasure will disappear, so he feels, with the cessation of his self-torment. Once again will he besmirch himself, rile himself up against himself, so he is again worthy of the punishment. He seems incapable of making restitution for his 'crime' because the crime is the pursuit of a pleasure. So is his sexual identity founded upon a sense of criminality.

The masochist's eternal, intrinsic guilt infects his entire sphere of contact, so he cannot touch anyone or anything without it becoming as filthy as he knows himself to be. The ordinary sexual embrace disgusts him, anyone who submits to his caress must have something wrong with them. He is attracted only to an unattainable, a frigid, cruel person: a Superior. She gives him the sense of immediate release from his sinfulness, for with the Superior may he re-enact the clarity of the parent-child relationship to crime and punishment.

In the chapter *The True Superior and the False* I emphasize the responsibility this places upon the Superior. The relief granted the masochist is rather like the lancing and draining of one pimple, when the source of the infected eruption is deep in the gut of the organism. The sadist treats only the surface blemish.

It seems the masochist is not born, but created by over-punishment as a child. That is, his sex-games, childish masturbation, or simple mischievousness regularly roused in the parent an anger all out of proportion to the misbehaviour. When a severe punishment is irrational, it is all the more deeply imprinted upon its victim. They continually refer to the parent in their minds, trying to 'figure out' *why*. They of course find no reason and come to blame themselves.

I viewed such a case, in a masochist who achieved orgasm during violent beatings. He traced his compulsion to the fact that his mother beat him regularly because she 'knew' he was masturbating. Almost anytime she came into his room it was to catch him. She often entered his bedroom late at night to 'discover him at it'. He was punished quite a few times when he had not masturbated at all. His sexuality was in this way subject to control by an authority and his self-stimulation and pleasure became identified in his subconscious with beatings.

The Superior ought to discover, when faced with a subject for punishment, whether the guilt feelings are specific or generalized. One may not expect to be too successful, for it is the minority who have come to terms with the lust for punishment. At best the Superior may hear a recollection of 'the last time' they went through their ritual. Rarely will one hear a recollection of a primal scene of punishment, when the association of pain with pleasure first occurred. The Superior may help the slave discover this original scenario.

Pressure should be applied to extract some semblance of a confession of the crime, for it is ill-advised to make up out of thin air scenarios of wrong-doing and punishment. This may only aggravate the feeling of the slave that he is 'bad', and creates still another reason for him to believe this is so: that he participated in a 'disconnected' form of degradation . . . he is so masochistic he will do anything. In order to relieve the pressure the scenario should approximate the earliest masochistic experience.

If the slave is a transvestite the Superior may use this confessional period to dress him in his female role, as he relates the history of his passion.

The second step after the confession has been heard is to merely look at the slave, and say nothing. You may find it enjoyable to hiss out one succinct comment, for example: "Vile!" — but silence is formidable. Stare at the slave, dressed in the rags of his self-contempt, and impress upon him your recognition — that you witness the reality of his criminal desire. These crimes may be nothing at all, laughable; that he looked at a girl's ankle and she caught him; that he wore women's underwear under his business suit. The point is that the slave is tormenting himself, and you need do little else but act as a resounding wall against which his guilt reverberates thicker and more intolerable.

Within this period of silence it is left up to the particularities of the case and the Superior's mood whether one looks kindly upon the slave-boy and strokes his head in a soothing fashion, or whether one requires he crouch abject in a corner and bear the full brunt of a stern gaze. He may be ordered to fix his eyes upon yours. Silence is effective, dramatically speaking, as it occurs here prior to the physical punishment, and so creates a definite suspense and contrast to what will follow. The slave is also enjoined not to speak.

Thereafter follows the spanking and/or the whipping. If a whipping only is to be administered, it is sometimes a good idea to precede it with a spanking to effectively prepare the buttocks for the maximum effect, i.e. render them red and tender and more liable to welt. Resonant as spanking is with childhood fixations, I will discuss this less severe form of corporal punishment first.

Spread-eagle restraint is recommended, as it prevents the subject from twisting the lower body away, and as well provides access to the inner thighs, a sometimes neglected and very sensitive area. The Superior will then reiterate the crowning indignities of his masochistic transgressions and sound out her absolute disapproval. Attention is then drawn to the helpless body of the slave, speaking of it as pathetic, weak, and unaware of what is in store for it. The punishment may begin over the underwear, and the excruciating humiliation of their being slowly stripped off can follow. The Superior may invoke an audience that observes this stripping, in imagination or reality.

Paddles are available to anyone in sex-novelty shops in major cities, as well as through mail-order. They ought to be tested before purchase, however, to see if they suit your inclinations. A slave may be brought along to the shop for this purpose — I doubt anyone there would object to a 'free show' of that nature. You will find many have a very flaccid 'hit' and are made of inferior leather. Such paltry weapons glut the market in an attempt to cater to a new breed of silly 'kinky' orgiasts. Novice Superiors beware. A good paddle ought to have some inner structure, a reinforcement of plexiglass, metal or leather. Paddles come long and thin, or round. The former permits the Superior to concentrate on small areas, while the round ones elicit an all-over glow. The unreinforced paddle is suitable for light punishment, but I consider the hand more intimidating and precise in that case. One paddle I used with excellent results was of thick leather reinforced with rubber, long and thin and bifurcate. This 'slapper' made a terrifying noise when striking home, and acted as a cross between paddle and whip, allowing one all the sinuosity of attack that a whip provides, along with the heavy-handedness of a paddle.

Of course the time-honoured favourite is the flat-backed wooden hairbrush. One creature favoured a few knocks with a rolling-pin, which he brought along in his briefcase with a very bizarre black ruffled apron — that *he* wore.

Of equal importance to the weapon used and the muscle-power behind it is the rhythm observed in delivering the blows. The bondage of the slave I again stress as essential — especially his head being rendered immobile — so he may not see the

Superior's arm as it rises. He ought not be able to prepare for the pain . . . so will the pain be increased. The Superior may begin with regular strokes and then vary them, faking strokes and missing a beat, letting a long moment pass with no attack, followed by a relentless flurry of blows. As the slave approaches his point of ultimate pleasure, however, and if this grossness is granted indulgence, the Superior may thereupon increase the heaviness of the blows and again regulate the rhythm, so as the buttocks are proffered the paddle forces them down again.

Let us say that a rather rough spanking has been administered, that the slave's backside has gone rosy-red and tender. The application of the whip upon this surface will leave very clear marks and may break the skin. So if this branding is not in order the whip ought not be idly applied thereon.

The best place to purchase whips, crops and canes is in a riding equipment shop. See to it that your salesman is an older gentleman, who will undoubtedly understand the special resonance of his wares, and may discreetly empathize with your intent. He will present you with the most charming little whips, nicely balanced, viciously precise, with handles tooled in gold. Whips are fashioned on the inexpensive side of fibreglass covered with a plastic weave. These quickly wear out at the tip and lack a certain responsiveness. The best are meant for heavy wear on a horse's hide . . . a particularly lovely one I possessed was made of one length of rolled and spiralled rawhide, four feet long, stiff yet resilient. One could just as easily flick and sting with it as bear down for a deep and penetrant welt.

Many are the accounts one may read of persons in jail, in hideous family situations, or of those who during the war adapted to the worst of conditions and submitted to normally unconscionable demands, though reacting at first with all the aggressive denial expected. This more-than-human tolerance of suffering and despair is experienced as a positive numbness of the mind and senses, a saving indifference to the real humiliating significance of their plight. This absence of affect is an emergency reflex that enables us to survive the worst insults to our humanity. We rarely elicit this faculty consciously; in an ordinary healthy existence it has little use.

In both the sadist and the masochist, however, it operates full-time. To assume the imperial stance of the Superior, or to allow oneself to be trodden upon are both reactions to a state of internal, emotional emergency. One wishes to control pain and suffering by invoking them; cultivating them as a test of physical strength, courage, and the capacity for self-denial, or imposing them under the auspices of a strict principle. Some may say: the trial would not exist unless you invoked it, and to this I respond: it depends on how deeply you wish to inquire.

The sadist, in actively inflicting suffering, determines the existence of suffering. Since he or she has invoked it, they are not its victims. The masochist, in wilfully embracing the suffering, and adoring his tormentor, controls what he suffers, what he has decided to suffer. The awful randomness of pain's descent is alleviated by his conscious desire for it. So here we are faced with the curious vision of neither sadist nor masochist being affected by pain, having set up their separate systems of control, yet both indissolubly connected with pain's evocation.

I hope I have demonstrated that whether one suffers or inflicts a flagellation, a suspension of ordinary consciousness for the sake of a mental 'one-pointedness' is the result. One might venture to state that both sadist and masochist are engaged in a form of meditation, in that the subduing of the body and its predictable reactions is the prerequisite of both. The practice has resonance throughout history, for example among the mystic ascetics of the Roman Catholic Church, who in deference to the spirit reviled the body, claiming thereby a purified perception of the Supreme Being. Their object of worship and the sadomasochist's objects are a 'heaven and a hell apart' — and I better appreciate those solitary devotees of the lash.

The masochistic 'criminal's' pleasure is slight for the duration of the punishment. For it is in the anticipation as well as in the aftermath of his punishment that the real pleasure lies. This may be understood in terms of the single blow, or the entire session of punishment. However with the Superior the pleasure is in the immediate violence done. The assumption of power over another is most exquisitely known in those short moments. As long as the Superior remains within the numbness threshold of the slave, the latter will feel *something else* through the pain, to which the pain is a means. So will he lay under the cruellest torture like one dead, and in this null state achieve his orgasm.

If a punishment is to be well-administered it should never be done in the heat of passion, out of fury. For the vengeance the Superior wields is an impersonal force. The Superior more truly resembles a type of minor executioner than a perverse, blood-thirsty specimen of humanity.

It is not up to the executioner to decide whether or not the victim is truly guilty; the subject has come down to her through a long line of convictions, the first and most telling of convictions being of course the victim's self-condemnation. It has been been recently documented in the USA, where in some states capital punishment has been reinstated, that the criminal desires to die at the hands of the law. His sense of wrong-doing can find no assuagement except at another's hands, and that other must be someone greater than himself. His private despair and desirable suicide turn a mean face upon him, he wishes to resolve his puniness and make of his death something grand; all his life's prospects have drained into the ignoble, and nothing less than mass hatred and execution can vindicate his will. Strange and inverted logic of the masochist, whose nobility is a great and ancient secret!

The evil, punishing persona of the Superior, an image that seethes with unrequited vengeance and strikes out against those who adore them satisfies the masochist's need for an impersonal punishment. He considers himself as simply 'getting in the way' of the violence he envisions as continuously emanating from the person of the Superior. He is therefore *not responsible* for initiating what he suffers — he tells himself this. Not any more responsible than one would be for falling in the path of a cyclone.

The Superior ought to recognize herself as a medium for a greater justice, the beginning and end of which she cannot conceive. Even to her this justice may seem too relentless. Her sensitive awareness of her power to remove guilt must be expressed in the conscientious use of technique. In the throes of his abandonment to this enormous natural force, the slave may awaken from his paroxysm to find he is badly beaten, which is one thing — but if he is still being beaten without quarter that is quite another. Those who favour severe beatings and tortures ought thus to submit only to an experienced Superior.

For when the slave whines, "Beat me with all your strength", what he means is, "Beat me to the limit, and perhaps a little more, of my endurance." Attack him 'til he feels again — and be done with it.

Torture

Superficially many signs of sexual arousal and rage are similar: there is a rushing of blood to the skin's surface, trembling, increased perspiration, grimaces and convulsive movements. Many dreams express sexual desire disguised as rage . . . the psychopath's repressed rage against women bursts out in acts of rape. Most persons when sexually aroused and entering the last stage before orgasm are able to suffer scratches, bites, rough and grasping caresses and vicious pinches without their being aware of the pain. Indeed this mild violence strangely enhances their pleasure. One is just as liable to inflict these blows in the paroxysm of sexual release. It has been my observation that masochists suffer from a peculiar pathology of numbness. All his pleasure depends on extremity; it is as if they cannot feel a subtle touch, cannot believe that contact is made unless it is violent and threatens them. The threat may be purely theatrical but in the context of the sadomasochistic clinch the theatricality is essentially real.

That the sadomasochist's capacity differs in degree from an ordinary person's tolerance of pain is only a partial explanation of the phenomena. For it is a physiological fact that the brain-centre that registers pain is exactly the same area that registers pleasure. This is why too much pleasure becomes painful; and too much pain, pleasurable.

Tortures have been used traditionally to extract information from the criminal or the enemy. Neither suspect nor spy are released until he gives his torturers what they want; nor is the slave released, that is, orgasmic, until he confesses to and suffers from his 'shameful' sexual trauma. As in psychoanalysis a patient relates a dream — in German, *traum* — so the slave spills out his disorganized, nerve-wracking traumata. A 'psychodrama' is then built up by the Superior around the extraction of the secret code, and with the possession of it she wields a great power over the guilty one — and will be sure to use it 'against' him.

Maximum bondage is advised. The basic tools for torture include: leather thongs, pins, stiff feathers, clothespins, ice, and candle and matches. More sophisticated tastes favour ready-made devices for the genitalia such as rings, chastity belts and cages, penis 'gloves' lined with pins, presses, small weighted shackles, tongs and clamps. For the true torture aficionado the Superior ought to have on hand: needle and thread, hammer, nails and a board, razor-blades, knives, liniment, pepper, and perhaps the electric prod of low voltage current available for just this purpose. Anything sharp and dangerous may be brought into play, including a dog's mouth and fingernails. Once in my experience a slave came to his absolute pleasure when I accidentally let slip a glass and it crashed to the floor. The cruel shards inspired me and I fastidously took up an edge in my finger tips. He caught the glitter in my eye as I contemplated the extreme . . . and lost himself.

The erectile tissue of the nipples responds in concert with that of the genital area. The reverberations from that area may be so intense the Superior may concentrate exclusively upon that area. The genital 'torture' would in this case consist of the Superior's ignoring the clamour down below.

The basic nipple torture involves first an oiling and light touching of the area, alternating bare hand with leather or rubber gloved hand. Next follows a little rude pinching and digging with the subsequent introduction of the favoured torture. Clothespins are the tamest form of clamp, and one usually begins with them, perhaps moving on to metal clamps with stronger springs and teeth. Place the clamps on the aureole so the centre starts out and makes itself available. Brushing them with a hair-brush when they are helpless like this, or teasing them with a nail-file is a mild yet devastating form of torture. From there may follow pricking, piercing or slashing with pins and razors. Piercing the nipples increases their sensitivity and may be imposed upon very submissive creatures. Lead them around by a little chain strung through the rings; leave the chain fastened to a post, and the slave's hands tied behind him. There you have a very simple, elegant bondage and torture combination.

The basic penis torture is based on a fantasy of castration, and the Superior will elaborate upon this theme with the 'psycho-drama' of the mad scientist experimenting on a guinea pig; of the dissatisfied lover taking revenge; of the strict and controlling mother or nurse-maid; any realized myth or fiction of the castrating woman. The penis and scrotum are observed as useless items — ugly, dirty, disgusting. Their only function has been to nauseate and perhaps frustrate the Superior. If there is an erection, it is invariably pathetic in its hopefulness — a joke, and small, very small. If there is no erection, the same abuse follows, coupled with the accusation of disrespect for not appreciating the unrivalled beauty of the Superior.

I will not go into any description of the abuse of the female genitals. Many women will agree that the act of normal intercourse is in itself a form of torture and an insufferable humiliation. This is a rather cool notion of the affair, but from this extremity may be divined that the act of rape, that is of undesired intercourse, is the basic fantasy for torture for the female. For variations on torture and abuse in this vein I refer the reader to the works of the Marquis de Sade who exhaustively applied himself to the subject.

The penis and scrotum ought to be prepared to induce the sensation of maximum vulnerability. A leather thong tied once around the base, brought round a couple of times under the scrotum and tied again around the base, and finally laced up criss-cross along the shaft, forcing blood into the end is a standard penis bondage. A thin rope such as Venetian-blind cord can be improvised with, but care must be taken not to tie a thin cord too tightly. A 'splint' can be created by placing a pencil, glass rod, or wooden dowel against the shaft and tying it there as described above.

The slave is then ready to be whipped, kicked lightly, tickled, pricked or frozen (the last performed prior to severe tortures for its numbing effect). Attach weights to the end of the bound shaft when the slave is in upright bondage to increase the restrained sensation. Bondage devices to constrict the scrotum, or stretch the skin of it may be attached, such as the penis-'glove', or 'jewel-case' — I would like to see this device made of glass, like a glass slipper, though to attach it to a prince considerably reduces him in stature . . .

For the most part it suffices to merely threaten the subject with an imminent emasculation, to gently and harmlessly glide a razor round the sensitive area, to strike an arrogant pose with knife in rubber-gloved hand. There is a mythology of the 'Nazi female surgeon' who will actually perform emasculations, that is, the removal of the scrotum, as well as mutilations. I once suffered the sight of such handiwork upon someone's passionately debased victim. His member had had a large slice cut all along the length of it, so that he possessed a kind of flap like a peeled-back banana skin, as well as a pathetically diminished working part.

Such extremes I consider beyond the pale and this example will no doubt evoke a shudder of revulsion in the 'novice' sadomasochist. You may well ask yourself, "What will prevent me from someday allowing the Mistress to do that to me?", or "What if I felt myself capable of inflicting the same?" One stereotype of the sadomasochistic proclivity portrays an irresistible decline, insists upon its being a degenerative disease of sexuality, and should one continue to indulge the most disgusting indignities will be suffered — or performed — with horrible, irreversible consequences.

Balance this point of view with the recognition that whatever gives pleasure may at times seem shameful and degrading; especially just after one emerges from the amoral frame of pleasure, and thinks over one's actions with a moral overlay. The prude is nauseated by the blandest sex . . . a husband is fed up with his regular-as-clockwork intercourse . . . the libertine turns in disgust from his whipping-boy. It is not the act itself that is monstrous — it is the mind that assigns the beauty or the lack of it that is so, uselessly imposing intense anguish and loss of pleasure through its confused workings.

Even so, in some persons the very 'repulsiveness' of the act will once again serve as the incitement to its recurrence. The only way to nullify this 'eroticism of disgust' is to divert, by a definitive act of the will, the loathed object of one's desire to the idealized object, and by that wilful decision deny the mind and the senses that particular satisfaction. It could mean temporary impotence but perseverance is all in this difficult undertaking. Alas, the slave — indeed almost everyone — is beyond taking themselves in hand this way. It may be up to the Superior to provide the stimulus in particularly destructive cases.

What would be such a destructive case? Wherever the Superior discerns the slave seeking out certain forms of abuse repeatedly and to the exclusion of all other forms of sexual contact. How would she provide the stimulus? Through overdoing it . . . through disrespecting his limits and taking the slave right to the edge . . . right to the logical conclusion of his obsession. For example, a slave came to me with his buttocks absolutely black from the beatings he had been paying for for over two weeks. He arrived with several paddles, all very heavy, of wood and leather, and studded in brass. One's initial reaction is to desist from aiding him in realizing his mania. It is important to try to talk things over with such a fanatic. But too often they must simply act through their ritual. I gave him his fill of abuse, and more . . . making a valiant effort to terrify him. But his capacity was for me unfathomable. He barely flinched throughout the entire hour of punishment which left me close to exhausted. Case-studies on the successful side are complex enough to demand a future study all its own and will not be delved into here.

One's ability to receive pain is not a finite circle, but as a spot of light increases in size, and its outlines blur as its source is drawn back from the wall, the subtle Superior may pull the submissive beyond his assumed capacity without his realizing it, with the elegant persuasion of her technique. A multitude of points exist within the sadomasochistic relationship, most succinctly evident during a torture session, where the Superior must make the choice between giving the slave exactly what he considers himself capable of withstanding, or asserting authority by going a slight touch beyond. The slave must place his absolute trust in the Superior.

The Superior notices the increase or the decrease in the slave's receptivity of pain by the same sign: a momentary withdrawal from excitement as the slave adjusts his pain-to-pleasure equilibrium. If the subject's threshold has been too speedily crossed, the balance sways in favour of pain. He will think of escape, and possibly become violent should the Superior idly continue on the same level of tormenting. Nothing is achieved through persisting in one's mistake — indeed, it serves to impress the slave with the Dominant's lack of control. On the other hand, if the torture was begun mildly, and the pain increased gradually as is proper, it sometimes comes to pass that the Superior fails to inflict enough pain. As the slave begs for more abuse, must the Superior feel herself under any obligation to accommodate this cry? What if they should feel themselves resistant, repelled by more suffering?

To challenge the frontier of one's capacity for sadistic expression, though frightening at first, will soon resolve itself, once the act is steadfastly perpetrated into the benign and innately wise indifference of the true Superior, for whom anything is permitted. Should you feel you cannot press yourself at that particular time, show yourself to be unequivocally contemptuous of his degraded lust. A slave often prides himself on his pathological indifference to pain, and enjoys the exhaustion of the Superior pressing herself beyond her limitations. So that unless you can meet and surpass the masochist's physical mortification, abuse him verbally and assure him you have seen much more submissive specimens in your time.

Mistress Angel's Favourite Penis Torture

Slave is thrown over an ottoman backwards, his hands and feet tied behind and away from him, so his torso is completely vulnerable and head is bent back. Take a thin leather cord and bind the member, winding the cord around the base and under the scrotum so it bulges out helplessly. Proceed with crossing and tying the cord to the end of the shaft where a loop is made. Attach weights to this loop so the erection is pulled down painfully from its proper direction. Attach light-weight clamps to nipples and abandon subject for fifteen to twenty minutes.

Your work will probably be all undone when you return, from the loss of excitement, so repeat process and go on to the rough play. Mistress Angel always enjoyed what she called 'target practice', flicking repeatedly at the crotch with a small bull-whip. Carry on any way that pleases you best.

Follow with the candle-wax torture, coating the shaft and the nipples first, then the sacs and the tip. Hot wax dripped along the sides of the torso is a fringe benefit not to be avoided. The candle may be held high so the wax cools a bit before landing, or held close to burn cruelly. When wax is completely dry, take a long, fine needle or perhaps a razor and remove the wax — each and every speck — taking care to stab the creature frequently. The wax ought to be removed from the nipples first, and crueller clamps applied. This will distract the subject somewhat from the terrifying procedure of the wax-removal below.

The effectiveness of this torture lies in the constant threat of extreme pain. The bondage need not be the strictest; the wax is scarcely painful if the candle is held high; the needle's proximity need never resolve itself into a direct stab. So the torture may be used for both light and severe sessions.

An interesting variation on the torture involves slashing the slave's parts a bit with the razor before applying in the wax and picking it off. This is assuredly an extreme torture, but many delight in the reopening of their wounds.

The Penis as Torture-Device

While a penis on a slave is always ridiculous, the same organ, whether artificial or real, is the object of the most fanatical worship when projecting from the body of the Superior. The phallus is forced into the body of the slave. Even if he can only accommodate the sissiest of dildos anally, he still is required to fellate a very large and ugly one. The Superior is never penetrated by the slave — the act of receiving the phallus, fist or foot of the Superior proves the slave willing to suffer violation. Though the dildo used by the Mistress has no sensation, it satisfies the necessity to pierce and use the submissive.

Dildos are fashioned of leather or rubber and made in sizes ranging from a little finger with handle attached for manoeuvrability, to a man-sized forearm complete with fist. Some have special built-in pumps to simulate ejaculation, others vibrate, or rotate by means of cranks. The Mistress uses these to subdue and humiliate the transvestite male, among others, or to bring a naughty girl to heel.

As discussed earlier, the genitals of the slave are a pitiable phenomenon regarded by both slave and Superior with disgust. Concurrent with his self-emasculation is his aggrandizement of other virile members, specifically that belonging to the Superior, who requires the slave to remain on his knees or belly so the phallus towers above, reinforcing his conviction of his servility to the phallus.

Among male heterosexuals the desire to know another man sexually, or at least to look at and hold another man's phallus is quite common though fraught with taboo. Under any stricture, the diversions of repression flower. The forbidden object of desire takes on an exaggerated desirability — in this instance, the penis becomes a kind of vengeful monster. The desire may thus express itself as the desire to be 'used', as he may envision himself having used women. He accepts the Mistress's dildo in an inversion of the heterosexual embrace; only in this way could he be said to be homosexual.

By the same obscuring logic he may dress up as a woman and wish to act as lesbian with the Mistress; or he will beg to fellate the transvestite maid, performing psychically an act of cunnilingus. He will only fellate a masculine homosexual *as a woman*; and usually only if the Mistress is present to observe and correct his performance, that is, to 'force' him to do it. All these forms of 'crypto-homosexuality' develop from the unfortunate idea that the nature of the homosexual contact is a degraded one, and that the passive male partner is a kind of humiliated woman. He may refer to his own genitals in such pleasant terms as 'cunt', or 'pussy'.

This noxious identification with a low womanhood is a masochistic masking of his dislike of women. He feels an aversion; feels guilty about his aversion; feels he should be punished for it; takes on the identity of the thing despised and receives punishment; so he becomes both punisher of the 'despised woman', that is, punisher of his homosexuality, and the *punished* woman. (In the chapter *The Transvestite as Masochist* I demonstrate how an identification with an idealized womanhood has its special difficulties.)

More dominant than his homosexuality, however, is his masochism, and he is certain to remain fixated in this state of receiving, but not giving, the pleasures due to homosexuality unless the Superior can sensitize him gradually to the fact of his distorted homosexuality. He may come out of the closet — but that is not to say he won't trade the stab of a stiletto for a kick from a motorcycle boot . . .

In male-to-male sadomasochism, the phallus-worship is less stylized and hygienic, more frankly sexual and brutal than the crypto-homosexual's pathetic joy in sucking on rubber. Gay men have made a cult of fist and foot-fucking, these limbs magically taking on the aspect of phalluses. The slave prides himself on how agreeably huge his anus can grow, how well-drilled he can become. The penis takes on a murderous aspect; the fantasy of being torn in two by a battering ram of a penis is not uncommon.

But it ought to be noted that one of the most effective forms of torture by the penis is to deprive the slave of all contact with it. He is permitted only to look upon it, as the Superior describes in detail what it could do to him. In this manner is the slave reduced to begging for his violation.

In preparing the slave for penetration, the Superior may build an appropriate fantasy based on the idea of Initiation. For the slave is to suffer the metamorphosis of becoming a Woman, degraded or exalted as the case may be. As such, 'she' must suffer terrible pain and humiliation. In all cases is the innocent introduced for the first time to a relentless phallus that will work its will upon the virgin orifices — engulfing and abandoning the victim to an excruciating, but delightful torment. Such scenarios may include: the Parent and Child (incestuous initiation); the Whore-Master and Prostitute; the School-Master or Mistress and delinquent Student; and finally the classic Superior and Maid-servant trainee.

Once the victim has been forced to take the phallus in mouth, or in the anus, he/she will manifest a complete turnabout and writhe like a slut in heat, insatiable for further abuse. (Unless of course the slave really is a virgin, in which case his senses will be rather pained and confused for a while.) The Superior is shocked to witness this behaviour, and berates the slave for lying about his sexual knowledge. The slave is severely punished for his shamelessness in pretending to be so innocent.

The most extreme of these fantasies of humiliation by violation is that of the Mother or Father, who is also a Pimp, taking their Child into a house of prostitution where he/she will lose his virginity and be trained to suffer brutal and repeated rapes by strangers. Thus will one stroke of the phallus be resonant with a multitude of defilements, in the de Sadean mode.

Verbal Humiliation

The techniques of verbal humiliation may be analysed into roughly three disciplines: first, in the development of the Superior attitude, as expressed through a strong and resonant tone of voice, proud carriage, impeccable grooming and a distinctive style of dress. The contemptuous words you let fall will be unquestioningly accepted by the submissive if he sees an aristocratic individual. Second, in the acquisition of the firm conviction that whatever one does or says in the presence of the submissive is correct and for a good purpose and shall be accepted as such. Third, in the cultivation of a relentless argumentativeness that will grind down one's opponent, bolstered by precise use of words, large vocabulary, clear and flexible diction, a familiarity with slang and coarser usages, and a fundamental indifference to winning.

Many slaves are oriented to humiliation by the word, differing from the fetishist who fixates on a certain sight. Contentious or patronizing conversation totally dominates them. Within this conversation is artfully wielded their 'magical' word or phrase that wounds them more deeply than any slap or whip-stroke can.

Volume is not at all important. The novice Superior seems always to be shouting, but losing one's temper is not really very dominating. More impressive is the restraint of one's anger, so that the submissive senses your fury building up behind a perfectly controlled and calm facade that will only gradually allow the full displeasure to be disclosed.

The Superior must learn to listen, in the midst of the gibberings and whinings of the slave, for *key-words* crucial to his dominion. These can be discerned by the awed tone of the slave, a certain fixed and wide-eyed look, by the repetition of the word accompanied by ecstatic shivering. Sometimes the slave will 'prompt' the Superior by saying for example, "Mistress, didn't you tell me I was a degenerate heel-sucker?" Such key-words and groups of words the Mistress elaborates upon powerfully resonate within the body of the slave and catch him up in the maelstrom of the *sounding* of his degraded identity.

The Superior uses the key-words sparingly at first, letting the sound and colour of the word fall like a drop of poisonous tincture into the disturbed pool of the brain. The saturation point will be reached in good time, and the Superior must take care not to administer an overdose, for too many refrainings cause it to din meaninglessly and drain it of all vitality, perhaps for a long time.

The twin 'sports' of sado-masochism and dialectic blend marvellously well one into the other, as both consist in main of attack and parry, search and revealment, defence and offence. Of course, in the former it has been decided in advance who will lose. This provides the predetermined winner, the Superior, with the pleasure of presenting extravagant theories and sophistries for the slave to meekly swallow, of forwarding any opinion as absolute truth, and of indulging in tirades and harping on pet themes to an eternally attentive audience.

The dominantly intellectual aspect of verbal abuse works most simply and satisfactorily with those of an education inferior to the Superior — though the masochist from the academic world revels in verbal chess-games. He will play fair — to his loss. There is a special pleasure in failing at what he is expert in, in the 'outside' world. Among these I include lawyers, whose verbal prowess is of the utmost importance. Impotency in verbal expression obsesses them and intellectuals as a group. That the Superior comes out 'on top', even when wildly irrational, creates such frustration and inferiority in the intellectual masochist — that you steadfastly refuse to come under the sway of reason. This is so very amusing, that the Superior's seeming ignorance controls and dominates him. Fruitlessly the slave will persist in trying to convince his Superior he is right. In this fashion is he forced to reckon with the limitations of his god, Logic. The Superior naturally understands and may agree with the slave, but to admit this openly is a fraternal exchange which is beside the point. Therefore one sees the necessity for the Superior always to be right, and that she remains unconvinced by all strenuous mental toil on the part of the slave.

Another form of verbal abuse is gutter-talk, the power of which is well-documented as a catalyst for sexual excitement. Crude ruffian language, the jargon and slurs of a bully, of a coarse and robust nature — under whose sway the simpering 'egg-head' has fallen — have a devastating effect. The Superior may use slang, ought to blur the elocution and above all chew gum as she speaks. Be lavish in the use of four-letter words, snicker when the slave cries and ignore all sensitive requests. One brings all one's theatrical capabilities into this affair.

The excitement here is of being dominated by a supposed intellectual inferior, who is psychically and perhaps physically stronger. Ignorance in the niceties of language renders the word-warrior impotent, his weaponry is blunted where a grunt passes for eloquence. He makes no contact with the Superior in the arena where he feels competent — and it may be the only context where he does feel so. As the Superior grows more laconic, he will usually become more talkative, making an utter blabbering fool of himself.

Here follows an anecdote drawn from experience to illustrate this phenomenon. The Mistress's English professor slave conversed with her on literature for nearly two hours. (It is a common occurrence that slaves may not immediately act as slaves but present themselves as important in some way.) The slave continually attempted to control the flow of talk by referring to authors he hoped the Mistress would be ignorant of, by breaking into foreign languages to confound her, and generally carrying on pretentiously — which may very well have dominated a less literate Mistress than the author. She successfully parried him on all points, except when she did not know a reference and he was required to recall it precisely, or when she did not know the material and he had to give a synopsis: all so she could say it sounded very dull, or was not a propos. Other than this sophomoric contention the discussion passed amicably enough. As the slave prepared to withdraw from his Mistress's presence, he threw himself at her feet — and she lavished upon him the most degrading compliments, elaborating upon his distinct debility of intellect, his pathetic attempt to impress her, his clumsy, third-rate vocabulary, winding up with her opinion that he was a worm-brained fake damaging the minds of his students . . . all this heavily spiced with obscenities from her store of foul language. I might add this session had begun with the slave enjoining the Mistress to 'tell me I am stupid'. So unfolded another masochistic convolute.

Many slaves enjoy psychoanalysing themselves and discussing their whole life histories. They often wish to explain to the Superior 'how' they came to be masochists. This is their way of showing their membership cards, to prove themselves 'real', and worthy of the Superior's attentions. Some may have interesting presentations and strike the Superior as persons of some will, concerned very actively in changing their ways. Others are too obviously shirking little weaklings, chronic complainers and spineless blabberers, who have so assiduously memorized their case histories they rattle it off like a soap-opera. One sees from their eyes they are not thinking — "How will this come to an end?" — but rather — "This is how I am, a big mess. Fix it for me. Isn't it awful and interesting and quite original."

In either case the Superior should see to it that the talkers do something, for example, submit at least to mild bondage. They must remain kneeling as they bore you. They are so accustomed to analysis without application you must impress them with the consequences of their lack of will. In some cases the Superior is well-advised to promote the image of the insensitive 'illiterate', who dismisses psychoanalytic jargon as over-complicated yammering, very wasteful and boring. Force the shrinking violet through the paces of a very strict submission, using scare techniques and threats of physical violence to silence him. To give him your ear is an indulgence he is stingily granted.

A Mistress associate of mine once very aptly described a

slave's talk. He had been feeling neglected and he telephoned her to 'whine at the top of his lungs'. Such vile irritations are to be expected from the slave — a certain verbal aggression coupled with an ineffectual attitude.

The Superior may discover in her stable crippled or deformed persons who are sick to their core of the veiled disgust and pity their wretched bodies daily force upon them. They find in the Superior a virulent honesty about the loathesomeness of their deficiency. It is at first difficult to be cruel to such unfortunates, but mindful of the imbalance one rights by so doing — of the hypocritical charity a normal person expresses when faced with a deformed person — the Superior will wield cruelty with the added consciousness of an impersonal force. Indeed, it is hilarious to say to a real cripple, after so many psychic ones, "What a pitiful cripple you are!" The beatific smile and relieved affirmation attendant upon this violence will reassure the Superior. The bald truth, without tedious euphemism, is a necessary food some may never receive, out of the misplaced delicacy and reserve 'kind' people practise.

Fantasies of Exposure and Abandonment

The slave is a furtive creature. Unless he is fortunate or wealthy enough to have continuous recourse to a Superior, the slave often makes use of pornographic and erotic books and films to sate his unusual desires. (Though some manage to eke out from the petty torments of daily existence a few precious drops of humiliation.) Aficionados of the 'peep-show' may develop their voyeurism to the exclusion of all other contacts. When in the presence of a Superior, so ingrained is the habit of *staring* to achieve orgasm they need never be disciplined for wayward paws. Voyeurism is generally rampant among masochists, so it is an accepted precondition that the Superior rarely has the slightest physical contact with the slave.

On the reverse of the coin there is the fantasy of being seen, and thereby violated by the Superior. In a typical scenario, the slave will be discovered committing a crime — usually masturbating to pornography — and he is reviled for this loathesome manifestation of his degeneracy. He stands shame-faced in the full regalia of his bottomless self-disgust, and is forced to undress in front of the Superior. This forced stripping is an excruciating thrill for him, as the Superior subjects each limb as it is unveiled to an appropriate sarcasm.

The fantasy of being exposed is made more extreme by submitting the stripped slave to the gaze of an audience, whereupon he is abandoned to their vicious commentary and made the object of more than mild fun. The Superior ought to insist that the slave pose in embarrassing positions, ask the audience to spit on him, whip him, do anything they like to him. He makes himself available, he abandons himself to the crowd — these sensations much enhanced when he is presented to them in bondage.

The Superior may put the slave into bondage and stow him away, gagged, in a closet, possibly provided with a crack for him to peep out of. He is told he must stay there indefinitely, that he is now part of the permanent household as the Superior's favoured 'bondage experiment' . . . or that until a use is found for him he will remain, like a stick of old furniture, forgotten in a dark cell. In this way is he both made secure, by being given a place near the Superior, and abandoned, by being ignored. He will spy on the Superior and other slaves, observing and unobserved, 'til he is again dragged out and cruelly exposed to a crowd. The 'peep-show' mentality finds pleasure in being left out of an exciting scenario — he places himself in it imaginatively, and may revolt against playing an active part. So the Superior's rejection of him he masochistically enjoys as central to his voyeurism.

Fantasy of Exposure and Abandonment: Dialogue between Parent and Child

The Superior, here as Father, discovers the slave, as Little Boy, abusing himself in a closet to pornography.

Father: *What are you hiding in the closet for, you stupid brat — oh. How beastly . . . (Tears the magazine out of the Boy's hands and peruses it with sounds of displeasure.)*

Boy: *Nothing, I wasn't doing nothing, Dad. (Tries to hide an erection.)*

Father: *Don't lie to me! I can see you — I can see what you're about!*

Boy: *You do not! I just found that book . . .*

Father: *(Drags Boy out of the closet by his ear.) Wretched little monster! How dare you abuse yourself that way! You're too young . . . I want to know where you learned such dirty behaviour! (Pulls the Boy over his knee and spanks him furiously.)*

Boy: *I swear I wasn't doing anything wrong! (Crying, still with erection.)*

Father: *Then what does this signify, I'd like to know? (Grabbing hold of the guilty party.)*

Boy: *Oh, ouch, please don't hurt me.*

Father: *Keep quiet. Make yourself presentable, your clothes are a sight. (Looks the Boy over long and hard.) I've been watching you lately, I've noticed something strange about you. I've been thinking I could see you had a dirty little secret.*

Boy: *You couldn't see anything!*

Father: *Don't talk back! I can see what you're about. (Slaps him across the face.) I've just found out. You're a nasty little peeping boy, ruining you health, looking at whores. Let's have a look at you. Strip!*

Boy: *No, no, I won't.*

Father: *Strip, I said, or else . . . (Produces a cane and thwacks the Boy viciously behind the knees with it. Boy speedily complies.)*

Boy: *(Moaning.) Oooh . . . don't look . . . oh*

Father: *It's just as I suspected. Look how you've degenerated already. What a puny chest! Do you think any of the sexy dolls in that magazine would put up with your scrawny boy's chest against hers? No indeed. Your arms are worse than a baby's. Take off your underwear. (Protests . . . punishment.) Just as I thought. It's shrinking.*

Boy: *It is not!*

Father: *It's shrinking, it's shrivelling up, it's going to drop off. I can see that.*

Boy: *I'm nude. (Tries to hide himself.)*

Father: *Get back here! You're nude. You're not going anywhere.*

Boy: *You're seeing me nude!*

Father: *Completely nude. You're so nude, I can see every inch of you. I can see your shrivelling crotch . . .*

Boy: *My crotch . . .*

Father: *I can see from the texture, from the colour of your skin, from your unwholesome odour you need my guidance more than ever. Every day you'll have to strip in front of me. You've been leading a disorderly existence . . .*

Boy: *Every day you'll see me?*

Father: *Every day. I can see you, don't try to hide.*

Boy: *You can't see me.*

Father: *I see you. I can see in your face the disorderly life you've been leading, all the disgusting dirty thoughts you've been thinking.*

Boy: *But I'm nude, I'm nude.*

Father: *Don't try to escape now. You're nude.*

Boy: *(Shivers.) . . . nude . . .*

Father: *Completely nude in front of me. What would your friends at school say?*

Boy: *Mother's not coming home, is she Dad?*

Father: *No, it's just you and your father, all alone.*

Boy: *Are your friends coming over, Dad?*

Father: *They're coming over to watch the game. I'll make you come in and bring us beers, in the nude.*

Boy: *No!*

Father: *I'll show my pals what a puny little boy I've got for a son. I'll force you to do somersaults in front of them. You'll pose in front of all of us and we'll stare at every inch of your nude body.*

Boy: *No . . . oh . . .*

Father: *We'll take you out into the country, all tied up in the trunk of the car. We'll ditch you by the side of the road, where anybody, a gang of teenage boys, will discover your helpless nude body, all tied up with your crotch completely exposed, they'll do whatever they like with you to amuse their drunken depraved teenage minds.*

Boy: *Will I be nude?*

The Pose: Etiquette of the Mirror

Following directly upon the inability of the masochist to have any true contact with his Beloved is his fascination with her image in a characteristic pose. The Superior may make use of all her theatrical ability without one gesture being lost on the slave. Perfectly acceptable within the context of the domination ritual is the Superior's spending an hour in front of the mirror, getting dressed, combing her hair, applying make-up and striking poses once dominantly attired — not for the pleasure of the slave but as a narcissistic exercise.

The Superior must take care to look only upon her own image in the glass. The slave will not dare look upon his own image therein, but only at that of the Superior in the mirror. He is required, throughout the time the Superior is looking in the glass, to look only upon this image in the glass, and not upon the proper person of the Superior. The Superior, on the other hand, rarely takes her eyes off herself in the mirror, and prefers to penetrate the slave with her gaze directly. Their eyes never meet, not in flesh, not in glass. For the slave there will be more reality to the image in the mirror, and so for the Superior more opportunities to psychically violate the slave — as he is observed continually in the flesh, is forbidden to meet her gaze, and when told to look is often instantly ordered to look away again. Should the slave look at himself in the mirror, or at the Superior in the flesh, he will be severely punished.

To look upon his beloved Superior is not a privilege the slave is automatically granted. He keeps his eyes lowered while in the presence and strives to earn the honour of gazing upon her. Every movement of the Superior is naturally infused with the dominating power. When the slave is briefly permitted to see her, he photographs every gesture in his mind, and thus the poses of the Superior come into the possession of the slave, struck indelibly upon the silver plate of his memory. The slave will later place himself within this photograph, with his favoured humiliating embellishment.

In a similar way does the Superior see the slave as a kind of resonating surface upon which her interior violence is realized. The slave's reaction is enjoined to be as subdued as possible, no screaming or thrashing will be tolerated. This control of reaction is especially necessary when the more vicious tortures are perpetrated.

In the ritual, only the Superior truly exists — in that she is the agent of all that occurs. Only the active part has reality; the passive, or reactive element occurs only in the masochist, and so has little or no substance and exists as a discard. It may be difficult to understand, but learn that it does not matter what happens to the masochist. He is a bottomless pit, into which any waste, or gold may be thrown — it makes no difference since it comes from the Superior.

The poses of the slave are exaggerations of the ignominity of his existence. The Superior requires first of all that he be physically lower than herself. His feet exist only to drag along behind him — or wave over his head like a helpless baby's. These poses as enforced by the Superior should be such as he would never find himself taking on within the precincts of normal society. These include crawling, wriggling on his belly, being bound spread-eagle, or frozen into absurd contortions for long minutes.

Any embarrassing position may be jelled through bondage. For example, when the slave is commanded to crawl while his wrists are shackled and his ankles handcuffed the crawling is very painful. Of course, if he remains in position of his own free will without bondage or repeated exactions so much the better.

The poses of the Superior accentuate the qualities of materiality, of relentless substantiality — unambiguous and rigid.

The legs are spread while standing, but the implications of the open legs are thwarted by the threatening footwear, the legs tightly bound in leather pants or an elastic skirt, the apex of the crotch rendered invulnerable in being tightly swaddled and enclosed upon itself, away from the eyes of the slave. Hands placed on hips, or crossed in front are both dominant poses, not tolerated in the slave. Why the hands should connect to one another or to the body is that the gesture works as a protective mechanism; one's physical and psychic energy is closed within a circuit that cannot be violated. So are the slave's hands kept at his sides, palms available, or stretched over his head and if behind his back they may not be clasped together.

The Superior ought never to lie down in the presence of the slave unless she is fully dressed, and the slave is on the floor beside the chaise longue or bed. She ought to rarely kneel, stoop, or squat — as though her knees did not exist to lower her.

The Superior poses as a living photograph for the onanistic excitement of the slave; the slave poses as a grovelling acrobat for the amusement of his beloved.

Under the category of posing comes the subject of costumes. There is some controversy as to whether the slave should be dressed, or not. If the costume is appropriately humiliating, yes. But for most interests complete nudity, enforcing the sensation of exposure and vulnerability, broken perhaps by a pair of underpants ordinarily worn by the opposite sex, renders the subject agreeably anonymous and ridiculous. The Superior of course remains always in costume, as nudity would reduce her to the pathetic animal, would level her in a way that is to be avoided at all costs.

The Superior succumbs to sensual indulgences in her preference for leather or certain materials. The pleasure, however, is not in adoring these materials on another, as with the fetishist, but in admiring themselves so encased. They may be attracted to another dressed similarly, according to the reasoning of the mirror-image. A slave has no right to wear leather; and a female slave's high-heels ought to be so high and tight as to cripple her, so her shoes are a form of bondage.

For the male homosexual costuming takes on a grave importance within the sadomasochistic ritual, not insofar as it separates Master from slave — as leather bars may be packed with slavish motorcycle cops, cowboys and construction workers — but in that it cues others to the fantasy they want to enact. Two leather-cops look equally threatening, are attracted to one another — but the pleasure is in the mirror-image and the struggle within that duality. Who will reveal himself as the strongest, the 'top man' . . . whose pleasure will reside in belying the image the fastest?

The same applies to two Superior women who come to grips with one another. The pleasure for each lies in the struggle for dominance, in the game of one-upmanship. Each attempts to subtly humiliate the other, and if one appears to bear the brunt of it most of the time, she will still wear her dominant drag — both as an incitement to further attempts on the part of the other to tear her down, and as a necessary re-assumption of a favoured role that sets her apart as an exclusive creature, separate from women as a group, intensely feminine and unafraid of what she wants . . .

The Superior may comfortably assume any costume that emanates the personality of an authority-figure. Evening gowns are always appalling, especially with jewels. A man's tailored suit and necktie is utterly intimidating — on the right woman. Military uniforms instantly subjugate — even the over-used and tasteless Nazi regalia. The image of wealth, of aristocracy or royalty ought always to be maintained by the Superior. The Master, through homosexual convention, may as well assume the rough-guy image of the blue-collar worker for the purpose of dominion over others. There is no equivalent for this with the female sex, though some men do find secretaries terrifying.

Cut-out leather designs, the obviously 'kinky' ensembles offered by sadomasochist supply-houses I find disgusting and suited for masochistic women only. In these clothes a woman reeks of available slut, which is precisely the role a Superior wants to impose upon a female slave or transvestite male. The costume of the slave might 'echo' the image of authority, as when he takes on the role of lackey. In Sacher-Masoch's *Venus in Furs* the slave-narrator describes how his aristocratic young Mistress created a livery for him, in her favoured colours. The lady of the house will always require a maid, and the jailkeeper needs his prisoner.

Fetishism

A fetish is an object that radiates a 'magical' field. It has no qualities of its own, or rather, its essential reality is held in abeyance, during which time it acts as the vehicle for the essence of the Superior. Whatever belongs to a Superior is not merely a shoe, a scarf, a garter, a letter — it *is* the Superior for the fetishist. Such objects become sex-objects for the masochist, who cannot release his desire in the presence of the one who permeates these items — unless she is wearing them. He can only express his desire with a secondary source.

Why a person becomes fixated on leather, rubber, nylon or satin; upon panties, boots, one particular dress or a style of trousers is not the inquiry here — but that they do, to the exclusion of all other forms of sexual stimulation is a subject for serious study by the Superior. For these fixations periodically require a recharging through contact with the Superior. If the slave fondles and adores his favoured item too long, without a renewing infusion from the magical source, the thing returns to its original and for the slave false and empty character. A stocking, for example, becomes a kind of rag permeated with his own effusions.

A fetishist is basically a sentimentalist. A little pair of worn-out shoes, a stained handkerchief, a withered bouquet or empty perfume bottle all have extraordinary value, in that they tap a memory. Recognize however that the memory your torn nylons evoke in the masochist are not only resonant of you and your recent violence, but are ikons of a person and possibly an entire series of events whose memory disposes him to a satisfaction so profound we may not wonder that the fetishist cannot be dissuaded from his fixation. For he kisses not only your shoe — by the medium of the shoe he kisses you and your cruelty towards him; he kisses all the shoes that ever dominated him; he kisses the shoe of distant memory that first dominated him and at last he may kiss the wearer of that first shoe: his first beloved. Perhaps this was a parent or parent figure, in which case the fetishist has anaesthetized the force of a taboo desire by swivelling before it a 'ridiculous' (and so to the observer, diverting) desire: the worship of an inanimate object.

Most fetishists come to the Superior with their tastes already set. The propensity of his mind to associate the sexual with the inanimate assures the Superior she may very well introduce him to another fetish. This would be instigated with the design of binding him to her in the present.

The Superior effects this by substitution of the one preferred fetish for another. One begins by teasing the slave with his favourite item, and when you have his attention quickly interposing the new material for his worship. Tell him he may not touch or look at his favourite until he humiliates himself with the new, that he must make this transference to the imposed fetish before his old acquaintance will be renewed. This may take a long time and requires the Superior's constant supervision and merciless insistence. But it can be effected.

What of the fetishist for parts of the body? The Superior may not be pleased to consider that in the slave's excision of one part of her body for consideration he effectively 'inanimates' it, separates it from her and her responses. In cases of fetishism of the breast, leg and so forth it is exceedingly important that the slave be denied and frustrated in his indulgence ninety-five percent of the time, so he is forced more and more to consider the Superior in her entirety.

During the training the Superior requires the slave's attention to be totally riveted upon the adored object. Let us say a Master wishes his slave to worship his thighs; the slave is then designated 'Slave of the Thigh'. The naming of the slave simultaneously gives the slave that part of the body, and takes away from him the possibility of 'possessing' another. Everything associated with the thighs is thereafter of great concern to the slave. If the Master has toe, foot, calf, knee and thigh slaves, these five will be responsible for putting on and taking off his pants, each smoothing the material over his cherished area, none permitted to trespass on another's territory.

Once the fixation has jelled through repetition of a ritual — that might involve washing, massaging, gazing, perfuming, kissing, paying compliments and so forth — the Superior begins to mete out punishments suitable to the slave's function. He will be forced to be present while another slave pays homage to his favourite shoes, or the foot. Most of the tortures will consist of the denial of favours once graciously imposed. The slave begins to beg, a sign that the fetish, like a stain, has taken. A severe punishment involves the slave being locked away for hours with only a photograph of the beloved object.

Irrational Fetishism

If one peruses Krafft-Ebbing one remarks the number of apparently unerotic objects of desire in the sections on fetishism. We can fathom the impulse to collect snippets of women's hair — hair is contingent to the body, is part of it, has familiar erotic qualities. As well the fascination with shoes and clothing — the garment evokes the part concealed.

But when the libido attaches itself to a wrist-watch, a ping-pong ball, a rubber dish; when a piece of cellophane from a cigarette-pack slowly crumpled with the words, 'I never want to touch you again' induces orgasm; when a Brooks Brother loafer crushing the corpse of a sparrow makes a slave's eyes roll back and his breathing shallow — we might well wonder what is this thing, 'sexuality' — and speculate but briefly before concluding that to restrict oneself eternally to one form of sex when the possibilities are so diffuse is like never leaving the neighbourhood one grew up in.

A slave presented me with a small chrome sports' watch and begged me please to wear it as he clutched my boot. He alternated kissing my boot with staring idiotically at the watch. He asked me to talk to him, tell him about the *time* he was my slave . . . for *how long* I was going to keep him . . .

Mistress: *You will stay here for several hours with me.*
Slave: *Time is running out.*
Mistress: *(Glancing at watch.) No, there's plenty of time.*
Slave: *You're keeping track of the minutes.*
Mistress: *Every minute you spend with me is like an hour. I think I'll go to sleep and let you watch.*
Slave: *I'll tell you when it's time . . .*
Mistress: *Oh . . . is it time yet?*

Slave: *The clock's ticking like a time-bomb ... (Begins masturbating.) You're going away forever.*

Mistress: *(Staring at watch.) The seconds are running out, there's no time left.*

Slave: *Please, more time, please ...*

Mistress: *(Counting backwards.) Ten, nine, eight ...*

Slave: *(Grips her wrist and rivets his eye to the face of the watch.) Give me more time, I swear, I'll make it up, I'll give you hours and hours ...*

Mistress: *(Snatching hand away.) I wouldn't give you the time of day.*

Slave: *Please.*

Mistress: *Time's up. (Slave reaches orgasm as she counts.) Four, three, two ...*

These cryptic references to time and his enslavement to me through time are utterly mysterious. The Mistress as keeper of time and so the controller of appearances and disappearances, versus the slave as time's victim, eternally waiting or watching things vanish is a highly literary conceit, besides its being a devastatingly erotic exchange for the masochist.

The Myth of Leather

Enclosed in heavy saddle leather, torn from the flanks of bulls, one is assured of a psychic as well as a certain physical invulnerability. What is more laughable than the weak of chin strutting in ill-fitting leathers? As comparably pathetic is the rich matron mincing in flimsy pastel and beaded hides. For it is not mere material, like silk or crepe de chine. Denim vies for a place on the throne near it, but it is too common, too cheap. Leather is inaccessible for a number of reasons, the one in main force being: it is the aegis of bestiality. A certain modern aesthete once remarked on the repulsive atavism of wearing another skin next to one's own. The ability to carry this emblem of the animal nature is the mark of a superior individual — it is a kind of overcoming — if he wear it well.

Black is the absolute sonority for the evocation of the oppressive sexual brutality of the satyr, the devourer within, whose senses unreined are the most destructive in existence. The restrained violence of the tanned and tamed hide we celebrate, let it stand as the cloak of imperial power as once did purple, unfurled cross chest and loins that do not flinch from saying: I impose my sensuality upon you.

The Shoe

In sadomasochistic practice the shoe vies with the underwear as most commonly fetishistic. Many slaves desire nothing more than to lie on the floor, to act as rug, footstool, or faithful dog so to be in constant proximity with the shoe. For the masochist the foot is not as erotic as the shoe, in that the shoe is a secondary source; its very unnaturalness, its distance from the Superior gives it its erotic value. One curious aspect of the worship of the feminine foot in high-heels is that a woman thus shod cannot walk very well — she is quite vulnerable on her stilts. Yet at her most 'tippable', her leg muscles their tautest she is her tallest and most treacherous. For the spikes are weapons and will protect her, a well-aimed kick will castrate.

Freudian symbolism equates the shoe with the female genital, by virtue of its shape and hollowness. From this one may see the foot as a masculine appendage. So is the shod foot a consummation. The spectacle of a silk-stockinged foot sliding in and out of a tight shiny leather stiletto-heel pump may suffice for a year's worth of 'shameful' paroxysms. The slave stares at this symbolic perfect fit, of foot in shoe, and adores it as something ineffable, quite greater than himself. He 'knows' it is very dirty and wrong of him to wish to have sex — it is impossible — which is why he passively, happily enjoins the shod foot to kick and trample him.

The heel of the stiletto is often regarded as a phallus. The slave is often interested in sucking upon it and being sodomized by it. At the other end of the spectrum is the naked foot a terribly weak little thing, that inspired in the Orient a cult of foot-worship. The foot was crushed to a lust-inspiring smallness and near absolute inutility; bent nearly in half to create a type of sub-vagina, a fold actually used by the male: so that a woman walked on her genitals, and not very far, at that.

Women manifest a fetishism for their shoes that men ordinarily do not. I collect shoes, and possess many pairs I have worn past any cognition of their original beauty. For some reason I cannot bear to throw them away. As well I favour tiny shoes, size three and four for women. I cherish besides a few pairs of my grandmother's spike-heels, all possessing for me the qualities of heirlooms. Each seems indissolubly infused with a heritage of feminine power. Stamped forever in my mind as proof of an undying and faithful love are the red spike-heels with bronze feathers my grandfather gave my grandmother on their twenty-fifth wedding anniversary.

The masculine foot attracts devotees by virtue of its grossness, its thick immobility and strong odour. The filthier the construction boot, the blacker and more massive the motorcycle-boot, the more menacing the man. The finality of the male's heavy tread, like the staccato clatter of a nervy high-heel, by the very extremities of masculinity and femininity they evoke impress the slavish mind with his vague and therefore ineffectual sexuality. Slaves may be seen to wear 'neuter' shoes, dull 'casual' shoes, soft and 'sporty'.* However, any shoe will do. One may be inexplicably aroused by a man's rather small foot in a supple, foppish Italian moccasin; and a woman in flat, thick-soled well-laced brogans gives off (for some) an irresistible air of horsy imperiousness.

The logic of foot-worship stems from the foot being the lowest part of the body; the slave as a low species therefore feels most comfortable in its presence. We have cast him underfoot and he is too spineless to rise — nay fears to, lest the weapon that is the cruelly shod foot rise against him. But there is more than this literal explanation.

In ancient symbolism the foot represents the subconscious mind, the darkest and most mysterious of our faculties. To beseech mercy of the foot is to ask of the subconscious release from the obsessive demon of unrequited sexual desire. The slave ap-

**The Sex Life of the Foot and Shoe*, by William A. Rossi, E. P. Dutton, 1976.

plies to the source itself, then — and in a more powerful being than himself. He would not think of kissing his own feet.

The slave begs his Superior to let him pay homage at the altar, at the foot, in hopes of receiving a sexual favour which is rarely granted. He in time fixates entirely upon the foot itself, and offers it countless sacrifices. Foot-worshippers are the most devoted of slaves, the most abject and touching.

In another context it was believed that in the foot of the king resided all his power, so that the foot-servant was charged with a near-mystical responsibility to relieve the very source of the kingdom's power from all onerous and mundane duties. His feet were never allowed to touch the ground. A European aristocrat's foot-servant replaced his Superior's feet with his own, and ran the tiresome errands. Still in another culture were the feet as well as the heart of one's slaughtered enemies devoured to absorb their courage.*

The foot is what takes a path, what carries one forward. The Superior's foot is not admired for this forthright quality, but is curiously still, made holy and perfect by the fetishist, shod in binding shoes reminiscent of the satanic hoof. Here we chance upon a resonance of the static and the death-worshipping in the sadomasochist's matrix.

***The Golden Bough*, by Sir James G. Frazer, New York, Macmillan 1951 (see chapter 51, *Homeopathic Magic of a Flesh Diet*).

Stockings and Socks

Male slaves, and I would venture to say men in general, are fascinated by the hosiery of women. Assuredly the stocking is the most ephemeral article of clothing a woman can wear. The stocking's combination of silky invisibility with delicate restraint quickens the slavish heart with its tantalizing irony. The flesh of a woman's leg is made firm, uniform and tense by a stocking. One can read in fetish magazines descriptions of women whose hose always seem to be pulled up and fastened so taut they are near tearing. This 'bondage', heightened by the skyscraper stiletto does not, unlike the bondage of the slave, render her weak and vulnerable, but makes her tense and vicious. The very painfulness of the extremely high heel ensures one a reservoir of useful irritability.

Those who worship stockings often favour sheer black stockings with seams, or black fishnet hose, resonant as they are of 'forbidden women'. Masochistic women whose Superior has a stocking fetish will wear white, though the Superior in her nurse's role will also wear white. In the former white represents virginity and innocence, while in the latter white is for hygienity and the strict purity of the authoritarian woman.

Often those who have a fetish for stockings are merely entranced by the silky feel of the garment. They will purchase stockings to play with, and may wear them around the house, luxuriating in the feel of the nylon or silk sliding between their legs. The sound of one stocking swishing against the other as a woman walks inspires violent excitement in the fetishist.

Feminists have a favourite cliche that represents the ultimate in degrading co-habitation with the male: they have to wash his socks by hand. If a woman will uncomplainingly do this she is truly submissive — or victimized by him, whatever the slant. The footwear of the male is malodorous and contact with it humiliating. The male or female slave of a Master will worship such filthy hose to prove they will do anything, that they adore his very loathesomeness. This practice impinges upon scatology, to be discussed further on.

Short white ankle-socks are representative of the child, and the slave-girl is often dressed in them to emphasize her childish ways and helplessness. In a strange case of regression a slave arrived with a special pair of pale blue booties a former Mistress had knit for him. Their being forced onto his feet was the highlight of his bondage session. The imaginative Superior may devise all sorts of games with stockings and socks to give the submissiveness of the slave stronger and more bizarre resonance.

Rubber

Rubber makes the body of the Superior strangely inert. All her outlines, crevices and bulges are exaggerated by the restriction of a rubber garment — pronounced, yet somehow lifeless. The slave worships the rubber-bound hand of the Superior, licks and caresses it in vain — no contact is achieved. The Superior unconcernedly hoses down when his paroxysms cease.

Inseparable from the love of rubber is the fascination with slime. For the masochist, rubber's sensuality is attendant upon a libation of spittle, urine, oil or a modern lubricant moistening the squeaky surface of the Superior's rubber garment or sheet. Rubber is better than skin for numerous reasons, in that rubber is poreless; there is no dissipation of the ooze that soils it, as with skin; within the rubber cocoon of the slave contact between his own exudations and those imposed by the Superior are indefinitely prolonged.

The dynamic contrast of filth with cleanliness, of disease with hygiene is the tension and so the excitement behind the rubber fetish. Rubber prevents the Superior from being infected by the all-pervasive contamination of the slave's presence. The slave's wearing of rubber forces upon him the loathesome proximity of his waste products. He is left in this condition for long periods; more on this love of wallowing in his or another's waste is detailed in the chapter *Coprophagi & Urinology*.

What then is the rationale for the Superior who favours wearing rubber? The heat of it, the protection, the appreciation of one's perspiration — I am not of this inclination so I may not speak lengthily upon it. A young Mistress of my acquaintance put on her tight black rubber blouse one evening and went out dancing with me. We had to repair to the ladies' room several times so she could pull it up and have me towel her off. She was soaking all evening, she said she felt clean perspiring so heavily: so the wearing of rubber seems to lend to one a faint tang of athleticism and by association, strength.

This same Mistress dreamed up the perfect rubber bondage for slaves. She envisioned a red rubber tube, slightly corrugated, into which the slave was slid as into a sleeping-bag. He then would have a red rubber cap fitted over his head, and *voila*! a perfect little worm costume.

Both rubber and leather being skin-substitutes they impress one with a sense of his naked skin's vulnerability. These materials create distance between the submissive and dominant — and I will reiterate the slave ought not to be permitted to wear leather, except in the form of gags, hoods, masks and shackles.

The fetishist for either rubber or leather may preen himself upon his super-sensitive, marvellously original and jaded sensibility — in that the ordinary naked body fails to arouse it. These rationalizations reveal the sadomasochist's revulsion towards intimate contact with a warm living body, one capable of a tumult of responses. For the masochist prefers one safe understandable response from the Superior, who feels most at ease expressing the same — contempt.

Fantasies of Bestialization

The desire to revoke the power of one's will and allow another to supersede therein manifests itself not only as the compulsion to become a contemptible specimen of humanity, or a helpless child, but in a further extremity of self-annihilation the masochist will destroy the possibility of rational thought and the power to choose what might be better for him, by reverting to an identification with what possesses only instinct: the animal.

Most common is the identification with those species that are domesticated, and are of service to humanity; the dog and the horse. The loathesome qualities of things invertebrate, of worms, jelly-fish and amoebae he may also joyfully assume. Thus does he create himself anew by regressing back through evolution; for even the regression back to a child does not suffice the desire to be unable to speak, see, or move as a human. He becomes a thing eminently crushable and crawling, dissolves himself into twitching, squirming blankness — that looks forward only to the descent of an irritated hand or careless foot.

The dog is unshakeably faithful, even in the face of repeated abuse. His four-footedness, his collar and leash, his dependence and the lavish affection he receives make the dog an object of envy for a slave without a home. The slave will whine and howl, and the Superior will have to walk him, though you may find yourself dragging the thing along rather abusively. The creature will never stop begging for marks of attention, and doesn't seem to mind if it's a slap or a caress —just as long as you notice it. Under no circumstances ought the Superior to tolerate a dog that is not house-broken.

Equestrienne training is preferred by those who enjoy more rigour in their bestiality. The horse will be outfitted with saddle, bridle, bit and stirrups, and the rider outfit herself in a complete riding habit. Spurs are a nice touch, and of course a crop or switch is not to be left behind. Such training involves more complex bondage (of restraint in which one can still move), less affectionate patting of the animal's head perhaps, more exertion on the part of the animal and the grave responsibility of his bearing the Superior upon his back. I have never trained a horse myself, only observed it done, so forgive me these few words on a discipline whose accoutrements and disciplines are complex, elegant, and worth an entire book to themselves.

Often a slave will desire to have sexual contact with a dog. This is a hideous degradation for the animal, and such a molestation I revolt against so exceedingly I would not countenance it in my presence at all. The verbal humiliation scenario of being forced to have intercourse with a dog or animal is much appreciated by devotees of verbal abuse. But some things it is not admirable for the Superior to act out, for even to look upon them is a kind of degradation.

Fantasy of Bestialization: Verbal Abuse of the Invertebrate

Slave remains silent throughout, nods his head in constant agreement and obeys the occasional command. He squirms about on his belly. The Mistress speaks:

You there, lowlife! Clean my shoes while you're down there! You're nothing but a worm, a worm beneath my heel. I've never seen such a loathesome thing, such an unevolved growth. Ugh! Detestable, how it wriggles around like that. It belongs in the slime, at the bottom of a garbage pail. That's where you were born, isn't that correct? From the slime, you disgrace to humanity. Did I tell you you were worse than a worm? Squirm, idiocy. A worm beneath my heel. It's so easy to crush a thing like you, spineless ooze! I hardly have to give it half a thought, and already it's crawling under my heel for it! You're really hardly evolved enough to be a worm. You're more of an amoeba. You're subhuman. An animal has more pride than you, you degraded specimen! What is that revolting appendage between your legs?

(Slave whispers his name for it.)

You call that a . . . ? What a joke. Do you know what I call it? A pathetic sort of growth that ought to be surgically removed. It's a sort of worm on a worm. It's more than I can stand, having two invertebrates in the room with me at the same time.

Don't you dare touch it! You let a worm control you? Oh, to think of that, that you are completely controlled by it! that it tells you what to do every minute, and you obey it, isn't that so?

(Slave pants his affirmation.)

No matter how degrading, or how revolting you make yourself to other people, no matter how subhuman an act it tells you to perform, you do it, don't you? Because you are absolutely out of control you have no will of your own, you have to be told what to do every second, isn't that correct?

(Slave breathes 'out of control' to himself in a kind of fixated ecstasy. The Mistress rises from her chair and poses over the slave, and she kicks him repeatedly in the crotch as she recites the litany:)

You freakish thing, you subhuman, insult to my eyes. All a vermin like you needs to survive is his lowest, vilest instincts, am I correct? You don't need to think, I'm arranging to have you lobotomized, my surgeon will drill a hole in your skull with her high heel. We'll have your worthless, rotten shrivelled excuse for a brain torn right out of your brain-pan.

And while you're on the operating table, we'll see to it that your testicles are properly disposed of. Then you will be a complete person, and fulfil your true destiny as an invertebrate itch! You'll thank me, then!

(Mistress resumes her seat and slave positions himself beneath it, so only his face is visible to the Mistress, just under her feet. The Mistress continues her monologue as the slave frantically masturbates; she rests her shoes on his face.)

Then you'll thank me, for then will your destiny be realized, subhuman vileness. Then you'll realize what you truly are, you'll know that's what you've always wanted to be in this life. You won't insult the eyes of women and Mistresses any longer, everyone will know you for what you really are, you won't be able to pretend you are a human being — a man! (She bursts out with a sarcastic laugh.) No more masquerade of walking around on two legs anymore, we'll all see you as the abortion you really are, a thing squirming in the dust Nature vomited out of herself in disgust.

(Slave begins to reach orgasm.)

You won't be able to trick women into having sex with you, either, every woman will smell you for the loathesome worm you are and become your

Mistress, every woman will be out to crush you. They'll take one look at you and know for certain, that you are a slave, you are spineless, nothing but a worm, a worm that's out of control, you are completely out of control . . .

Coprophagi & Urinology

After the slave has fantasized himself as an animal, a pet, then a worm and a subhuman, he may evolve to impersonating furniture, or to becoming invisible. But his pride drives him on to more absolute identification with lowliness. His inverted logic seeks to turn him into a submissive beyond all others, a slave among slaves. He attains this end, and becomes ineluctably disgusting, when he professes his ambition and attraction is to be as one with the faeces and/or urine of the Superior.

These substances, regarded as horrid by all, are revered and sought after by the masochist as the source of his true identity. His contact with them strengthens his resolve to be the worst of men and the best of slaves. It is very peculiar for the Superior to realize these slaves worship her waste products more than any good quality. But this is typical of the slave, who aspires to so little. The Superior takes scant pride in such slaves, unless she regards her products with the same glamorized eyes as the masochist. Her waste becomes the lowly one's nourishment; her filth cleanses the slave; her foulness is a rare perfume. In this poor way does the slave ingest, and so possess something of his beloved Superior.

It is held that a piece of bone, flesh, or even a scrap of the shroud of a saint possesses all the qualities of blessedness that the living saint emanated by their will when alive. To touch such a relic is to receive a jolt, as it were, of the power once harboured by the living body of the saint. Power does exist outside oneself, that one may draw upon and make manifest, through concentration upon a relic as a focus of power. The power that heals, however, does not reside in the relic itself — which is a sort of fetish item — but is drawn out by the believer from within himself, the relic acting as a catalyst for the believer's power of self-healing. But the relic possesses nothing in itself.

The masochist seeks out vileness — his identity — through his concentration on what is commonly accepted as the vilest substance on earth. But faecal matter is the raw material for all that grows on the earth — it is no more wonderful than it is disgusting. Autistic children have a fascination for their waste products, for in their ultra-egoism this substance that comes from their bodies possesses all the distinction of a creative achievement. They cry to see it flushed — the slave meticulously prepares a cocoon of plastic sacks and boxes to carry the Superior's precious response home with him.

The slave deifies these substances, giving them names such as 'golden elixir', 'shower of sweetness' and the like. He may ingest them or merely hold them in his mouth for a spasmodic instant before spitting them out. This behaviour creates such revulsive contempt in the Superior the slave must be ready to do absolutely anything the Superior thereafter commands. But the Superior may be at a loss, for it seems no degradation can surpass this one.

Concurrent with this love of filth is the slave's toilet envy. How perfect would life be if he were installed in the bathroom of the Superior, made a permanent fixture therein, on the spot at all times to receive a dose of his beloved communion. The toilet slave enjoys being referred to as 'toilet' or 'sewer', and in the case of a transvestite coprophage, 'Latrina'. He may be left happily chained to it for hours. In the case of a slave who pays a professional Mistress for this pleasure, the designation 'john' takes on a special resonance.

Both the scatological fetishes are most illustrative of the fact that fetishism is a form of necrophilia: a love and attraction for what is dead, decayed or disappearing.

Coprophagi & Urinology: Filth Dialogue

Scene takes place in the bathroom. Slave is chained to the toilet and lies on the floor. Mistress is perched upon the sink.

Superior: *How many gallons can you drink?*

Masochist: *As many as you will give me, Mistress.*

S: *You are a toilet —you love being a toilet.*

M: *Yes, yes, anything you say.*

S: *It's true. Your highest ambition is to be installed in the ladies' room at Grand Central Station.*

M: *Will you watch me clean out the urinals with my tongue?*

S: *Women don't use urinals, fool.*

M: *I'm sorry, Mistress. I'm just a toilet.*

S: *You're the type who thinks it would be heavenly to have hundreds of strange women squatting over your face, using you as their sewer. Admit it, vileness.*

M: *It's true. Please, Mistress, let me kiss your ass, oh my beautiful Mistress, let me eat your . . .*

S: *(Kicks him.) Don't say 'my' Mistress. I own you, thing. As for kissing even the bottom of my shoe, your mouth is too dirty. Who knows what you licked today, the gutters you crawl in, so shamelessly. I don't want to catch your diseases, you disease!*

M: *Please Mistress, use me as your toilet, piss on me. I want to eat your shit.*

S: *Silence! Keep your degraded lusts to yourself. Besides, my products are too good for you. The food I eat is very expensive.*

M: *I'll pay, I'll pay.*

S: *I know you will. I ought to have a little porcelain bowl installed over your revolting orifice. I don't care to sit down on moving objects. Let's see how wide you can open. Wider! (Inserts her heel into his mouth.) Lick it!*

M: *(Salivates all over shoe, whining.) Please Mistress, I want to be your toilet!*
S: *Greedy little pig! I told you to lick my shoe, not eat it! (Takes a long time cleaning her shoe.) Now, you were saying you wanted to serve as my toilet. That this was your true place in life. Perhaps that is all you're fit for. But you have to learn to move up in the world, to earn your privileges. First you must prove in other ways how useful your mouth is. Clean the floor! (Holds his head down with her foot.)*
M: *Mistress, please, it's hard to lick the floor when you're stepping . . . ooww . . . (Tries to peer up her skirt.)*
S: *What's this? Complaining? And oh! On top of it all! Looking at my legs! I don't let my servants look at me while they're working!*
M: *I apologise, Goddess. I couldn't help myself. Please forgive me. (Sprawling abjectly on the bathroom tiles.)*
S: *Get back on your knees, spineless! You need some discipline!*
M: *Oh no! (Watches in horror as the Mistress fills up an enema bag with steaming hot water.) Please, please don't, I'll do anything!*
S: *Then you'll take an enema! You do as I say and nothing else. Stop pawing me, animal!*

(The Mistress requires the slave to present his buttocks to the air and keep his head lowered as she administers the douche.)

S: *Now, that ought to clean up your act. Let's have a little entertainment around this place. (Unchains slave, puts on a record and forces the slave to dance for her. If he is a poor dancer he may be egged on to improve with a few licks of the whip.)*
M: *Mistress, Mistress, I beg of you...*
S: *You let one drop fall on my carpet out of your sorry little ass, and you'll wish you had never been born the slave you are!*

(The Mistress may, if she thinks the slave can tolerate it, have him run a few laps around the house, preferably hopping on one foot.)

S: *Hup, two, hup, two, exercise is good for you! (She yawns. Slave is by now grimacing in pain which delights the Mistress immeasurably.)*
M: *Mistress I think now I am very cleaned out...*

S: *Silence, toilet-boy. Kneel over there and wait for me to notice you. (Mistress amuses the slave by telling a story of how severely she punished a slave for letting a drop fall on the carpet.)...and I thought that would teach him how to have a little more self-control.*

M: *Oh darling Mistress please may I go to the bathroom?*

S: *No.*

M: *Please, please, may I go. (Mistress does not bother to answer.) PLEASE I HAVE TO . . .*

S: *(Strikes out with the whip.) YOU DIDN'T ASK ME 'PLEASE MISTRESS'.*

M: *(On his knees and trembling all over.) Please, darling Mistress.*

S: *You have permission. (Slave starts to run . . . Mistress screams.) Come back here! Kneel down.*

M: *Yes, darling wonderful Mistress, please, yes...*

S: *You didn't say 'Thank you, Mistress'.*

(Etc. Finally the slave is permitted to relieve himself. When he emerges twenty minutes later he looks very ashamed.)

S: *That should clean up your act once and for all, you degraded little beast. I'll teach you to look at my legs without permission.*

M: *Yes, Mistress. Mistress?*

S: *Ask my permission to speak!*

M: *Mistress, may I speak?*

S: *No.*

M: *(After short pause.) May I speak, Mistress?*

S: *What IS it?*

M: *Won't you please use me as a toilet, Mistress?*

S: *No, I don't need to.*

M: *May I serve you a drink, Mistress?*

S: *Very well.*

(Slave hurriedly dons an apron and prepares a drink at the bar. The Mistress receives the cocktail; the slave stares fascinated as the liquid courses over her lipsticked lips. The Mistress puts the boy in a stocks so he won't be bothering her.)

S: *Now amuse me by singing a little song, you must sing 'I adore being your toilet' to the tune of 'I Adore Being a Girl'. Now keep singing! (Slave sings this one line, tunelessly, over and over. Mistress laughs restrainedly.) What a stupid little creature! So tormentable.*
M: *I adore being your toilet, I adore being your toilet, I adore being your toilet, I adore being your toilet, I adore being your toilet, I adore . . .*

(Mistress takes slave out of stocks and presents him with a drink. It is her golden shower in a glass, which he is forced to down. Slave sips carefully.)

S: *What if I had a tub filled to the brim with piss, what if I shoved your head under 'til you soaked it all up, you'd be saturated! Just like a nasty little sponge!*
M: *(Guzzling.) Oh thank you divine queen, thank you . . .*

The Transvestite as Masochist

Popular opinion will assure you that all transvestites are twisted closet-case homosexuals. However, the majority are heterosexual fetishists for the sensuality of female clothing; within their ranks exists a spattering of transsexuals, who are preparing to take on the female genitals as well as the female costume. Both admire women so inordinately as to deify them, and themselves wish to take on the physical, and thereby magically the emotional and spiritual qualities of the revered Goddess. To dress up is their ultimate pleasure, to imitate the Mistress their devout obeisance. As a rule they are not severely masochistic, and enjoy such naughty-girl punishments as spankings, scoldings and doing the laundry. They wish to be delicate, 'girlish' and sweet, their masochism expressing itself as a feeling of frailty and helplessness, which the Mistress may pleasurably take advantage of.

The Mistress will quickly learn to distinguish between the homo- and heterosexual aspects of transvestitism. The healthy homosexual transvestite, that is, one who admits her attraction to men, and chooses to attract them as a woman is more likely to be dominant than submissive. The famous shrewish 'Queen' may be supremely virile in bed with a man. Her sickly homosexual cousin is discussed at length in *The Penis as Torture Device*. With a male transvestite Superior, the crypto-homosexuality of the transvestite slave is peculiarly apparent, as an illusory lesbianism is enacted by both men.

The unhealthy homosexual transvestite, who always acts out the slavish role, wants to realize himself as a degraded woman, and will appreciate the sluttiest of ensembles. His cross-dressing, usually 'forced' upon him, is his way of assuming a masochistic persona. In his inversion of reality, he considers women (among whom he is one) in the conventional negative light so he may be crushed too. The Mistress stands aloof from his general poor opinion of women in a strange and just vacuum, as the slave relinquishes his own power and projects it onto the Mistress — who is then as flawlessly dominant as he normally considers himself to be. She may be the only woman he grants power to — the one to whom he has 'lent' his power — and he can only respond to her power as a degraded female.

Transsexuals are drawn to the Mistress during their transition from male to female. They present a relatively simple problem to the Mistress, as they want not so much to tear themselves down as to build themselves up. Yet as society holds the attitude, still, that a woman is a low creature, the pre-operative transsexual sometimes comes to the Mistress out of confusion, to be punished for wanting to be a woman. Under the Mistress's instruction they try out different feminine roles, often that of maid or adolescent girl. They are taught how to use make-up, how to shop, told where to buy clothes for women of their build, taken outdoors dressed up to see if they can pass as a female — in short, the Mistress helps the transvestite build up a good positive image of himself as a woman, and continually bolsters his confidence so he is not plagued by guilt. However, it is inevitable that guilt will arise, and the Mistress is there, too, ready to mete out strict bondage, punishments, and verbal abuse. This symbolically alleviates the subconscious residue of guilt and helps the slave to feel he has been punished for his indulgence, while enjoying his indulgence — all under the gaze of the Mistress.

These men are very conflicted and unhappy about their ambiguous sexuality, and their masochism may be aggravated by the insensitive Superior who fails to make a strong effort to treat the transsexual and transvestite in all respects as a woman — and to impress upon her that to be female is good. All of them need to look to someone for a creative reinforcement of the feminine role.

The ritual of dressing the slave as a woman ought to be lingered over, and great care and attention given to creating the most perfect possible image of femininity. The Mistress will note that as the illusion accumulates on the physical the male takes on an entirely new set of gestures and voice intonations. 'She' is given a woman's name, and corrected when traces of former virility distort her movements. She ought to be encouraged to talk about her female persona — when she first became aware of it, how she deals with it each day, how she views herself as a woman in relation to others (they are often lesbian).

Transvestites are the most amenable of submissives in that they are very conscientiously working this conflict out and often see the Mistress in conjunction with psychotherapy, for she permits them to act out their fantasy as well as talk about it. The Mistress takes on this responsibility in all seriousness, having on hand a wardrobe of wigs and make-up to experiment with, black 'risque' underwear as well as virginal white, outerwear for elegant women, for flashy tarts, for go-go girls, secretaries, maids, orphans and little school-brats.

That the Mistress encourages the transvestite to discuss his fantasy is very important, especially in the case of the simple fetishist who may think himself seriously perverted. Many are married men in dangerous daily proximity to the tantalizing froufrous of their wives. He will not reveal his fantasy to her for fear of rejection. The wife of such a man aggravates his desire when she expresses a fearful disgust towards his interest, and punishes him worse than any whipping could.

She ought to realize what a great compliment it is that he identifies so strongly with her — it may be that he very innocently delights in the feel of delicate materials next to his skin, a pleasure largely denied men by convention. Women who make men feel 'perverted' for this identification with femininity must have a very low opinion of themselves.

The Superior helps the transvestite realize how reasonable his fantasy is, how tame and commonplace compared to others. In time he may be able to persuade his wife to give in to him. Of course this presents another difficulty, as he is basically a submissive person and fantasizes that his wife initiates the dressing-up. For him to *ask* her to force him is too dominant a role for his taste.

In short, transvestites of this fetishistic bent are the least unfortunate of submissives, as there is nothing basically harmful in wearing women's underpants, as opposed to having tacks pushed into the penis — though penis-punishment is logical for transvestites, who may come to despise their sex. But the fetishism rarely usurps the 'normal' sexual drive — it is an eccentric flourish. Transvestites may turn masochistic because they feel no one accepts them.

Transvestite as Masochist: Dialogue between A Mother and her Daughter

The slave is wearing slut-drag: a trashy, cheap, revealing dress, torn and dirty underwear, a sloppy wig and too much make-up. The Mistress wears a cocktail dress, nylons and heels; her hair is pulled back in a severe bun. As Mother, she enters her Daughter's bedroom. Daughter is covertly masturbating.

Mother: *Theresa! What are you doing!*

Girl: *Oh, Mother . . . I'm sorry, I didn't mean to sleep late.*

Mother: *Shut up, you little sloven! You were supposed to have been up hours ago! The house is a mess, and the girls are due in an hour. And just look at yourself.*

Girl: *I can't help it, Ma.*

Mother: *Don't talk back! Get up this instant. It makes me sick to look at you lolling there, still wearing the clothes you had on last night. I suppose you passed out as soon as you came in? And why was the bed jiggling when I opened the door?*

Girl: *I don't know, Ma . . . I'm sorry.*

Mother: *You certainly are. (Shoves Girl out of bed onto the floor.) You got stinking drunk last night, and not only that, you got yourself all worked up, sitting outside the house for an hour in your disgusting boyfriend's car! Don't think I didn't see you!*

Girl: *You did not! I did not!*

Mother: *Fresh hussy! (Slaps her face.) Don't you dare contradict me! You were masturbating.*

Girl: *I WAS NOT!*

Mother: *(Slaps her several times.) Little liar! I'll teach you to lie to your*

Mother, and to behave like a slut, sitting where all the neighbours could see you!

(Yanks Theresa back up on the bed and sits on the small of her back and administers a rough spanking by hand.)

Mother: *Beg for my forgiveness.*

Girl: *Motherrrr . . . please . . . forgive me . . .*

(Pretends to cry.)

Mother: *Shut up, you bore me. Now get to work.*

(Theresa hulks about listlessly, her clothes dishevelled, half-heartedly dusting. When she is told to clean the bathroom she begins whining.)

Girl: *Don't wanna.*

Mother: *You pouty brat, you slop, you think you can get away with talking to me like that? I ought to lock you in the bathroom until it's spotless. Though a dirty girl like you would be likely to make the bathroom slimier than when you started!*

Girl: *You meany! I'm going out. Johnny said*

Mother: *(Interrupting.) What? Go? GO WHERE? JOHNNY SAID?! (Punches Theresa in the face in her fury.)*

Girl: *(Crying her head off, that is, pretending to.) MOTHER! It's not fair! I'm eighteen and I have a life of my own!*

Mother: *I certainly don't know where you learned such idiotic things. You have no such thing as a life of your own. I want to know how a cringing piece of trash can think she has any say on any subject. Take a look at yourself! (Drags Theresa to the mirror.) Why in the world an ugly girl like you with her fat legs will wear purple fishnet stockings is beyond me. It's bad enough you're as huge as an elephant, but with those wretched stockings you force everyone to look at your stumps!*

Girl: *Johnny likes them.*

Mother: *You dare mention that fellow's name to me again and you'll wish you'd never been born the slut you are!*

Girl: *Oh, Mommy, why are you so mean to me?*

Mother: *Don't tell ME what to do!*

(Mistress ties Theresa's hands and feet together with rope, pulls down her panties and spanks her 'til she weeps.)

Mother: *On top of it all, your panties are a disgrace.*
Girl: *I'll be good Mother, please let me go.*
Mother: *Stop whining, and try to behave, the girls are here.*

(The Mistress then pretends there are three other women present, all with distinct personalities, invented for the purpose of the discipline that comes later. She humiliates the slave before them and speaks to them. Only an experienced Superior ought to attempt such a piece of acting, as her powerful imagination must evoke the three not only for herself but for the slave. There are: Jacqueline, a very mean lesbian, who gives the most heavy-handed punishment; Anne-Marie, rather sweet and submissive but a bitch all the same; and Madame Rose, an elderly Madame of a house of ill-fame.

Mother settles herself at a table set for four. Theresa goes around, pretending to fill the glasses, bringing in empty plates for them and a full one for her Mother.)

Mother: . . . *it was getting very late and I was growing very angry when at last a car pulls up. I looked out the window, expecting to see Theresa stagger up the walk — she's such a delinquent, she's been drinking almost every night — but I waited for over an hour for her to crawl out of the car! (Listens.) No, I wasn't about to go out there. I might have seen something that disgusted me too much. (Eats, listens, nods.) Well, of course they were having sex which is strictly forbidden her. Isn't that how most of your girls got started, Rose, having sex in cars? (Long silence as she listens to the women talking. Slave fumbles a glass and Mother glances at her sharply.) Oh, the creature is a kind of hoodlum, very good-looking, greasy hair, tight pants, truly a degenerate, the sort that forces young girls to fellate them in the back seat of a car.*
Girl: *Ma, don't tell them that! (Squirms excitedly.)*
Mother: *Tell them what, that that's what you did? Shut up, trash. Do you see how she talks to me? (Listens.) I agree, it's a disgrace. I hope we can get this marriage arranged soon. Do you think a rich old man like that will be able to handle this over-heated tart of mine?*
Girl: *I won't get married!*
Mother: *You'll do as you're told. Bring in the coffee.*

Girl: *I'm not a virgin!*

Mother: *(Stunned into silence. Then:) What was that?*

Girl: *I'm not a virgin! I won't marry someone you pick out! I have a life of my own!*

Mother: *(Drags Theresa by the ear viciously to the ground and kicks her in the stomach.) Oh! This is the end! Ruined! You heard what she said. To think I have been trustingly harbouring a prostitute in my house! Next thing you know she would be bringing her tricks to her bedroom! A life of your own, what a joke! From this day forward you belong to Madame Rose, who will use you in her basement as you deserve to be used. You will be bound and gagged and forced to serve only the most revolting clients.*

Girl: *NO! HELP! I WON'T! JOHNNY, SAVE ME!*

(Mother and the girls lunge for Theresa and drag her into Madame Rose's basement. They discuss among themselves the tortures she will have to endure, as they tie her spread-eagle to a rack.)

Girl: *Let me go, I'll tell Johnny and he'll kill you.*

Mother: *Go ahead and try to get in touch with that weak worm boyfriend of yours. From this day forward your only human companionship will be your tricks. Johnny's probably off in Lover's Lane right now with a different slut and you're the last thing on his mind. Yes, that's right, Theresa, to him you're just a used piece of Kleenex. ('General' laughter.) Now Anne-Marie you start, break her in with your little hand that's still learning how to hit. Oh, you're tired already? Well, now it's my turn, to let her feel this. Okay, Rosie, it's your turn. Give the tramp a taste of what's in store for her. She's going to have to service sadistic men! Now Jackie, go on and whip the living daylights out of her!*

(Mistress inflicts the punishments as she speaks, pretending to be four different women. She may use different voices; the slave will beg differently to each. Each personality has a specific attitude, each increasingly severe. Punishment ends with Mother beseeching 'Jackie':)

Mother: *Jackie, darling, please do stop. I know you're crazy about my daughter and can't stand the thought that she's going to be ruined by men . . . it's her fate, her downfall . . .*

Jackie: *She's such a ripe little tart, I got carried away. Remember though how bad Anne-Marie's brat got it last week?*

Mother: *Do I ever. Delicious.*

(Daughter is untied and permitted to masturbate as the Mother ignores her and talks about whipping children. Slave reaches orgasm in a few strokes.)

Transvestite as Masochist: Dialogue between the Prostitute and her Pimp

The fantasy herein enacted involves the young Prostitute and her female Pimp, or Madame. The Prostitute wears Cleopatra eye make-up, very sluttish, is decked out in platform shoes, sleazy blouse, see-through panties, fishnet hose — all the trappings of her degraded status. Keep in mind the young Whore is a middle-aged man in drag.

Madame: *Now young lady, I suppose you understand what is expected of you now? Why you have been brought to this house?*

Whore: *(Cringing, eyes downcast.) Yes, ma'am.*

Madame: *Your behaviour at the convent was so terrible the nuns felt your true vocation was here, in my House. You're going to work out very nicely for me, aren't you, dear?*

Whore: *Yes, Madame.*

Madame: *I expect more enthusiasm than that! (Threatens girl with a whip.) I wonder if you are fully aware of what I expect from my young ladies?*

Whore: *I really want to give blow jobs.*

Madame: *Ugh! What vulgar language! I won't have my girls talking like that. Grotesque! (Forces Whore to her knees.) I expect my girls to be ladylike at all times. (Shoves Whore's face into the carpet with her foot.)*

Whore: *Begging your forgiveness, ma'am, I need control.*

Madame: *That's evident. Kiss my foot nicely and perhaps I'll let it pass. (Whore passionately embraces Madame's leg and tongues it lustfully. Madame kicks her viciously in the face.) I said, kiss nicely! You've got to learn to take orders, when it comes to sex! What a hungry dog you are. No class at all!*

Whore: *You see how much I need control. The nuns were always whipping me.*

Madame: *Tiresome, so tiresome it must have been to whip an unrepentant thing like you. I can see why they threw you out!*

Whore: *I wouldn't confess to the priest. But they all knew what I was doing . . . why did I have to confess?*

Madame: *(Swacks her whip against the Whore's flank.) Confession is a sign of repentance, that's why! Don't question your Superiors! Confess to me now, you squirming slut, tell me what your qualifications for this job are. (Whips the Whore throughout confession.)*

Whore: *(Running around room and squealing.) I went around . . . to everyone's bed . . . at night . . . I would sneak under the covers . . . pull down the girls' panties . . . I played around with . . .*

Madame: *That's enough!*

Whore: *. . . I seduced the Father Superior . . . I was forced to service all the nuns once a week in front of the entire school . . . the Mother Superior was jealous . . .*

Madame: *(Gives one last severe cut.) That's quite enough! Well, by this confession you have proved to me the only life you're suited for is that of the whore.*

Whore: *That's what Mother Superior said. She was really mad at me. She loved me.*

Madame: *Don't flatter yourself. She'll be getting a cut of all the money you'll be making here.*

Whore: *No! I won't give it to her!*

Madame: *I know you won't. I will. (Looks through notebook.) It says here you have almost too much experience as a lesbian.*

Whore: *Would you like a demonstration?*

Madame: *Forget it! Here you have to learn how to satisfy a man.*

Whore: *Yes Madame, whatever you say. (Grovels to the carpet and fondles herself.)*

Madame: *There'll be no masturbating here, either. I'll have to restrain you. You have to keep all your excitement for your clients.*

(The novice Whore struggles fiercely in her bondage to no

avail. She only succeeds in arousing herself. Madame begins to punish her slowly, gradually working up to a severe whipping.)

Madame: *Now, my darling, you are well-primed for your first customer. You must learn to be a brave girl.*

Whore: *(Snivelling.) Yes Madame.*

(Bondage is changed so Whore now lies on her back, heels over her head and immobilized, so her derriere is completely accessible.)

Madame: *Look at yourself now, look how you're behaving! You're grotesque! Did you think your playful games at school would bring you to this? You are heading for total degradation. Anyone who came in now could use you anyway they pleased. They could fuck you, rape you, violate you like the worthless piece of trash you are, just as though you were lying unconscious in the gutter.*

Whore: *As though I were lying on the sidewalk on Times Square . . .*

Madame: *As though you were a Times Square prostitute, you'd be abused 'til you had no mind left.*

Whore: *I want to be raped, I'll do it, let me work the streets. Tell me to do it.*

Madame: *I don't have to tell you to do it, you'd do it anyway if I didn't keep you in bondage in my House. I require only one thing of you, that you let your clients do absolutely anything they want to you.*

Whore: *Oh yes!*

Madame: *You ought to be thankful you can work in a good House like this, that I don't force you to service the lowest of the low . . .*

Whore: *But that's where I belong.*

Madame: *Since you want brutality, I'll send all the sadistic men to you.*

Whore: *Thank you, thank you, I'll worship you forever.*

Madame: *What a disgrace.*

Whore: *I'll make a lot of money for you. Give me the biggest cocks, the roughest trade . . .*

Madame: *Stop shrieking for it, I know you're crazy for a man.*

(The Madame forces a dildo into the slave-girl's rear and affixes it so that it cannot be ejected. A large dildo is then repeatedly thrust down the Whore's throat.)

Madame: *You want more than anything to be violated, you love to be used, you love to be completely submissive before a man, you'll do anything he tells you and thank him for ordering you around . . .*

Whore: *I'm working for you . . . I'm working for you . . .*

Madame: *You may now consider yourself a completely used thing. You have been broken in. You are a piece of merchandise, ready for the market. But I wonder if I am going to be able to make any money off you. You're already so worn out.*

(A strange transformation of role then occurs, where the girl-Whore becomes a boy-Whore, though he is still dressed up. His attraction to a man becomes the frank attraction of a man to a man.)

Whore: *You can always turn me out at the Anvil, Madame.**

Madame: *You'll suffer the worst degradations there.*

Whore: *I want to dance, I want to suck a hundred cocks in one night, I want to lie down in the urinals.*

Madame: *I'm still not sure they'd put up with that sluttish mouth of yours. I might have to pay them to have anything to do with you.*

Whore: *Don't you think they'd like me to perform for them?*

Madame: *Who in their right minds would want to look at a little slut like you? You don't care, though, you're so wild, you'd get the chance to see a bunch of naked men.*

Whore: *Wouldn't they pay me? I'm really hot. I think I already know how to give blow jobs really good.*

Madame: *Your grammar is despicable! You have no class!*

Whore: *I want to get fucked on the stage...*

Madame: *They can get all the sex they want for free. They'd be in disgrace if they even let their piss touch you.*

Whore: *I'll do a strip-tease...*

Madame: *You'd be better off in one of the trucks parked outside. You would be tied up, spread-eagle like you are now, helpless on the floor of the meat-truck, lying in the slime. You'd like to lie on a filthy floor and get raped like a carcass . . .*

*The Anvil, famous New York City homosexual sex-club.

Whore: *(Masturbating.) Yes . . . yes . . . a motorcycle gang . . .*

Madame: *A motorcycle gang would park right by and glance in the truck and see your helpless little ass waiting for use. I'd be there and I'd invite them to go into the truck, for a dollar, to go wild all over you.*

Whore: *They'd squat . . .*

Madame: *Yes . . .*

Whore: *They would all be wearing condoms . . .*

Madame: *I doubt it.*

Whore: *I would suck the juice out . . . (Comes to orgasm.)*

Madame: *You're very perverse for a novice Whore.*

Two Fantasies of Special Interest

Often the masochist acts out through his chosen profession the dynamics of control and punishment. Certain professions seem to require an appreciation of, if not a definite taste for sadism or masochism.

I once disciplined a very strangely sentimental masochist, whose session began with an elaborate formal interrogation, outlined for me at our first meeting. I played the part of some 'German Officer' in boots, cap with insignia, leather trenchcoat and convincing accent. (He described his true profession as that of 'special government agent' — and it served as well as his fantasy profession.) The punishing interrogations he enacted upon 'the enemy' he claimed evoked in him memories of his mother's severe inquiries into his sexual behaviour, and the punishments that always followed. He felt her interrogations predisposed him peculiarly to the sadistic methodology of his profession — in the practice of which he found: identification with his mother; control of her by assuming her role; revenge against her, through punishing others; and to confuse things still further, intense sexual gratification.

After his capture, interrogation and bondage for an hour in jail, his mother came to retrieve him. The confession that the German officer had extracted was a fake, his mother told him. But he was being released into her custody. I released him from bondage, and we pretended to be going home. The mother then began questioning him concerning any homosexual contacts he might have had while in prison. These inquiries became very detailed and insistent, and the son finally confessed to his mother that he had been seduced, had enjoyed it, and that he'd do it again if he had the chance. The mother then whipped him soundly, berating him for his 'perversions' the while, and again was he placed in strict bondage and left 'in the basement to think over his crimes'. So was he re-captured into the chains of a submissive boyhood.

The case of the police vice-agent is truly classic. He knelt before me and confessed to harassing and arresting prostitutes on the streets, claimed he brutalized and insulted them, and often forced them to service him sexually, with promises of release from the charges which he later betrayed. Once put into bondage, he proceeded to insult the Mistress, promise her an immediate arrest once he got out of bondage, swore he'd rape her in a jail-cell, and such like, as I went on silently whipping and caning him with some pleasure. As I persisted he calmed down and became exceedingly passive and 'feminized'. He begged me to please help him get a job where he could serve women to make up for his crimes. His special fantasy seemed to be that of boot-boy and laundry-boy for a professional lady-sadist.

Quite obviously his chosen profession exacerbated his sadism past his toleration, so in order to 'save' himself psychically he fled into a masochistic bouleversement. Though he usually preferred to be at the mercy of a woman for his punishment, the extreme guilt he suffered from led him on one occasion to enjoin me to assume his role.

I dressed in a man's suit and tie, and became him: the vice-cop, allowing myself to be picked up by 'her'. He was completely dressed up as a hooker, and had all the gestures and little phrases down. We went to a room and she solicited me for money. I whipped out my handcuffs, threw her down on the bed and told her she was under arrest. She promised me sex if only I wouldn't, please. So was he humiliated as he had dirtied hundreds of women. She promised to work for me, and give me all her money — and when I agreed, she went into such paroxysms of pleasure it was clearly demonstrated how he envied the pimp.

Obvious in this case is his hatred of his job, his recognition of its brutality and hypocrisy, and his continuation in it because he is a masochist.

The True Superior and the False

The Superior for one cringing slave is not the Superior for another. One must accept in many cases that one's dominance cannot radiate in its full power. One is tempted to ironically observe that one's power depends upon the depths of the slave's submissiveness — but I tend more to the opinion that the brazenness of the sadistic ego determines the liberties the masochist will enjoy. But human authority is never a fixed quantity, immutable in all circumstances.

The truly submissive male, for example, sees all womankind as his Superior. He in his devout subjection would never dare insist that the Mistress have only blonde hair, wear only certain clothes, or recite a fixed formula for his masochism to be satisfied. He asks only to be included for a moment within the circle of her supreme contempt for the male. In every woman he finds the beauty and charm that becomes, for him, her cruellest quality. Thus the confirmed slave never knows the pain of a false Superior, as nothing a woman can do or say is wrong. Even should the Superior degrade herself, he in turn strives to make himself lower.

False Superiors are those who permit the specific masochism of the subject to control their control; they rarely do what they really want to do, but accept a scenario and play a role for the masochist's pleasure. They are not true sadists, they have no ideas concerning control of behaviour, no real interest in subtle punitive techniques, no interior command to rule others and be served. True submission unquestioningly accepts the programme the Superior sets out. For the Superior is a sensitive being, and he or she well comprehends in a brief exchange with the slave exactly how to reduce him to jelly.

The Superior role will aggrandize one's self-esteem. But if the role deflates when the slave departs, something is very much amiss. In such a case the Superior assumed no real authority. By 'real' I mean: spawned by an internal necessity to rule. The travesty of authority will be indulgently suffered by the true devotee of male or female Supremacy, but with slaves who have not yet developed a strong consciousness of their servitude, such play-acting and dependency upon 'cues' presents to his untrained mind the depressing spectacle of a degraded ideal. His submissiveness may be spoiled by this falseness as well; many times have I come across slaves who claim to have been 'submissive' for years who won't stop talking when they're told to. This falseness is something of a relief to some masochists, I think: his desire to indulge in truly masochistic behaviour he realizes is being *catered to*; he may relievedly reassume a 'dominant' role, tell the 'girl' what to do, and so postpone his acid-test.

In the professional sphere where many masochists begin their training such false domination is rampant. The professional Master or Mistress exists in a limbo whose boundaries are marked by prostitution at one end — hence the 'catering' syndrome — and by psychotherapy at the other. Their function closely approximates that of a nurse or physical therapist, though it verges often towards that of jailer, or keeper in a mental hospital.

If the professional Superior too much identifies herself with the prostitute, which occurs as the 'business' of domination is on the books as illegal, she may fail to have any respect for herself which will be her downfall. To look down on oneself in this way is to act as a hypocritical society would have one do.

The author feels a very strong identity with the psychotherapist. This seems to be the highest function of the Superior's role in society, that of relieving the pressure of arcane sexual needs. At one time I believed I was curing the masochist, but this was specious and an egoistic justification. There is no cure, not even in non-indulgence. Non-indulgence is repression; repressions are only more or less successful, and not forever. When they are less so, the sexual need reasserts itself. It is the last stop in the psyche, and like the process of defecation in the body, the orgasmic expulsion relieves and cleans the *mind* of waste. I have little scientific background to make such pronouncements; I speak only from my observations and experience.

The inexperienced masochist does not yet know his place, and he wants to. He feels it is at the foot of his Superior, but he feels inhibited. He wants the orgasmic solution, but what is the question? He is furtive, guilt-ridden, and worried about exposing his secret desire. When he at last is able to confess to his masochism the Superior must be prepared to take complete charge. They must not disrespect the confidence and must instantly impose the rigorous structure within which the slave may be a slave. He is required to obey, and the only demand the Superior will tolerate is: Master, Mistress, do what you will. This demands great trust from the slave, inasmuch as he does not really know what designs the Superior has for him. The design is, of course, only that he be able to realize his masochism as fully as possible.

If this trust the slave proffers is taken lightly, as it may be by the prostitute 'playing the game of S & M' one assumes the risk of aggravating his guilt intolerably. The masochist trusts that the Superior has the power to elicit his hidden desires, help him express them, and remove the guilt from them: that the Superior accepts, and perhaps even approves of his masochism. Only the true Superior is capable of inspiring this, while the play-actor will in the end be found sneering at the slave as 'sick'. The inexperienced and disrespected slave will turn on such persons, attack, and attempt however poorly to dominate them, because he feels they are laughing at him, the ones in whom he placed his sacred trust.

I am always amazed when this trust is given to me, a complete stranger. I feel nothing but respect for the bravery of the masochist in submitting to his desires, in my care. Even the inexperienced Master or Mistress can assure themselves against the delicate problems that arise in the sadomasochistic exchange by rigorously maintaining the appearance of a true Superior, and working continually on perfecting its truth. The voice need not be raised, or angry, but cool and even and emotionless. The gait is graceful, slow and assured. Dark and concealing formal evening clothes are never unintimidating; severe unadorned styles being more imperious than the flashy. All coarse easiness of manner must be eradicated. She is a flawless lady, and a highly moral creature; he is a gentleman, subtle and passionate, who brooks no laxness of character. Neither are at all tolerant of the failings of others.

The Masochism of the Superior

The masochism of the Superior is evident: if they were not masochistic, would they submit to the fawning of a slave? Would they suffer his whining? Would they permit such imperfection to violate their environs? Yet they do all this, and without feeling victimized — stoically do they admit their masochism, without *exhibiting* their humiliation. A lesser man or woman would soon feel persecuted by the slave's cries for attention. The true Superior recognizes, however, that the worst violence or degradations they impose upon their slave they could and would in turn suffer. But they restrain themselves; this is the only reason they are able to inflict the sufferings.

It is next to nothing to satisfy the slave — one need do very little to exact their obedience — for the submission flourished full-blown in the slave's mind, before he ever met you. He torments himself well enough. If the Superior attempted to kindly fulfil all the whimpers for abuse they heard soon would they become slaves in turn.

For masochists are devourers, little vampires, voids — they cannot be sated. I am as vicious as possible, I am very understanding — it makes no difference. Both intents are sucked into the vortex of their selfish craving. At certain uninspired moments I have felt to be even peripherally involved with the begging demons is a draining torture like no other.

3

Tourniquet

Under the thrall, the melodic spell, the sway of an irresistible order, I let myself fall, my eyelids fell over my exhausted eyes. For one moment my thwarted sight searched the membrane of the inner lid, then ceased its fretful ricochet. Nothing at all to see, at last. I bid my eyes turn and gaze in, and up, into the roof of my brain. By a sudden swerve of the imagination I rotate them back another ninety degrees 'til I see out the back of my head. Held there they briefly flutter as though trying to escape.

For one moment a static, then a shrill obscures the brain's screen — then a black emulsion engulfs me and without warning or willing I plummet through an unknown and sunlit terrain, cross mountain ranges of annihilatory grandeur, up to the face of a vanquished wall, in whose gatehouse dwells the solitary, spectral observer. I see roads, long and empty and silent, roads just barely travelled, desolate yet compelling, twisting off into the unyielding distance of a morose countryside.

I stop at the foot of the wall, well out of the observer's sight. He knows I have arrived but nothing else. I wish to remain indistinct for as long as I can. Wordless, I survey my foreign expanse of rock and friendless path, summit and swooning crevasse . . .

Then my eyes close again and nothing at all is evident. A serene profondeur floats me into the funnel of something slowly churning through a fluid, unplumbed hush. Sluggishly am I buoyed along within this dreaming sea-denizen, whose ever-open maw feeds on all that drifts in its path. The soft, powerful engine of its fathomless belly digests celestial constructs, degenerate dogmas — all prickly pairs into a smooth and malleate paste.

I gave way to an encroaching unsettlement — I was alone in the torture chamber. All the lights were out and I sprawled on the rubber sofa, enveloped myself in its crumpled, resilient surface. Tucking my ancient leather jacket beneath my head, I lounged, turned my spike-heels prettily this way and that in the dim four o'clock light, dreamed stupidly of a patent-leather dress to match them... idly I mark the time, watching reflections from the passing cars glide cross the aluminium-painted ceiling. I had drawn the shades and along their plastic edges the daylight glared.

I started playing my game, the one I made up when I was small, 'making monsters'. Its pleasure is you never know what the outcome will be — what the monster will look like. First, stare at an object long and fixedly until it begins to lose its form and solidity. Intone its name over and over to speed up the process... whereby the object is transformed into an abstraction, an alien construction of colours, shifting angles, pendant spheres, texture and scintillating light. It then happens that with one's eyes wide open the object disappears. Remain suspended here; a sudden thrust, of fear, or will, then jerks the object back into sharp focus

— not as it was — but into its true shape. True? Yes . . . the false husk's off, and 'tis unfailingly a hideous thing.

The object so reduced, I draw it into myself — that is, upon its transformation I draw into myself the knowledge, now visible, of an inexorable dislocation. I am neither able to know nor to understand anything at all of this world, and that is a right I may enjoy. I see there is nothing worth knowing, except this passionless flicker that cuts the eye from the hand. In this limbo I bask, glory in my arrival from another planet — muse that I am deep in the embrace of some silent psychosis.

I will end my days in an asylum, and I see myself, between my violent rages, idiotically staring at random light patterning the drear walls that will enclose me. I will not recognize them as light, nor as reflections or shadows, but as things in themselves — curious and friendly personages, characters from books I cannot recall reading, or new, paralyzed enemies. I will not be able to say, as I may now — that yellow blur on the ceiling is made by the sun shining on a taxicab roof. Such ordinary relief will be denied me.

As a cloud broke the thwarted sun showed brilliant round the edges of the plastic shades. My unease distilled itself, as I stared and stared at this light. Its reflection, cool and diffuse, glimmered upon the ceiling. I tried to suppress my breathing, I listened . . . The radio came to life, after feebly buzzing between stations for an hour . . . a dull rock beat emerged. In the deep cold blue of the walls I bathed, my body swathed in the mingled clean odour of latex with musky leather. Through the rigid atmosphere imposed by the air-conditioner a waft of alcohol drifted. Was I in surgery? I stared, I was in a trance . . . all at once the daylight on the ceiling went out, as though night had inexplicably fallen. I panicked and the light clicked back on, and I saw what had been daylight was precisely the colour of fluorescent light, most artificial of lights. These bands of harsh white at the shades' edges I now realized as neon tubes hissing out hard constant light. The walls moved in nearer to absorb and throw back the cold in its deep blueness.

I sensed my chamber as deep underground, penetrable only

by some sibilant steel elevator. The air-conditioner gave a mechanical snort, as if suppressing a malicious hilarity, then started up again with a great groan and clatter. Over and over it purified my air, this air of the underground vault — what muck lay in its belly! — keeping scentless my hermetic atmosphere. I burrowed deeper into the elastic comfort of the couch, and as once more I realized my dark security, I had the sudden inspiration to know myself inviolate as a mummy, sealed within a forgotten crypt.

The disappearance of the windows, the false shades, the daylight faked by neon, and the plummeting underground of my room — all these visions clarified with a tremulous finality my embalmment of myself in the role of the Superior.

After almost an hour's silence my business line rang. Before 'good afternoon' fled my lips I heard, as from a great distance, the recorded voice of a man, metallic and earnest and in mid-sentence: ". . . . to examine your conscience. Your actions must be in imitation of Jesus Christ our Lord, and you see how you have failed in this. Do not weaken, do not despair, you will come to know His love for all those who have strayed from the fold. He died for your sins in the Name of His Father, and so by prayer will your soul be renewed in the Light of His Love . . ." The voice clicked off.

I heard the message through in a sort of stupor. The voice droned, had a disgusting compulsive lilt to it, this stupidity increased by its recorded nature. Yet a dullness in me embraced it. But the repetition of 'you will', 'you must' irritated me, too, and I sneered, a little late, "I will not."

I felt I had to recover from something. Those familiar phrasings, resonant with the manias — once known as devotions — of my childhood had succeeded in provoking from out of my prevailing melancholia that vague urgency I so dreaded.

What had drained devotion to make it mania?

Who had played the message? It was a trick, a sick joke. What was I afraid of? That I was damned? But you've known that for years, I spat at myself. Too late to start whining now. It's just the

Christian con, they're in the same racket as you, control of base emotion . . . you're in competition for blood's why they go after you . . . their attack is just another form of the justice you are subject to, swallow the medicine bravely and shut your trap . . .

I threw myself back into the maw of the couch. The neon tubes resumed their original though not correct appearance. There again seemed to be a window behind the shades I could go and look out of, if I wanted to. But it was not a true sight, whatever I saw out there. I turned up the radio and was alarmed to notice how joyous I was. Someone had considered me sinner enough, in grave enough danger, to call and preach at me! I stared at the ceiling, as a sudden reddish glow infused the white radiance reflected thereon. I was devoid of fear. I was prepared.

The integrity of my criminality! A perverse and inunique ideal. Should one at heart a suicide, intent on the grinding of the spirit to fodder for a wild beast (who appreciatively shows his teeth at each reopening of the wound) dare speak of something whole? I feed it when it's hungry, no matter what! It is my beast...

I have long been aware that I no sooner place two sticks side by side than they uncontrollably cross. My mere presence inspires others to behave perversely, in my shadow flares the contrary. Nothing so simple as some baby's 'integrity' survives the company of the monster — round me all is complex, mysterious, known by half... swallowed in a miasma that seems romantic but may be only vague.

Strange and demeaning to consider my great Evil, my fatal, precious stigmata may be nothing but a mistake, some ill-conception. To destroy my victim soul; to devote myself to this purgation and purification; to wrestle an antic will to heel; and to contact and be assumed into the company of the Elect — all these intentions have degenerated to a species of pride, dissipating to the accompaniment of an insipid whine. Moist and lax of spine, I cringe at the truly strong's approach, and so despising my smallness I devise a virulent horror to shock and sicken.

I will not . . . I refuse to make any distinctions 'between right and wrong' . . . it's all the same to me, I want as much as, want all of it . . . Am I really spineless, isn't to draw this line tiresome. Yet I am on the line, and so drawn is my world quartered, clearly . . . no path apparent. No, I refuse to do it. You cannot force me! I like my own good, my own evil, I oversee setting them at each other's vitals, stand idly by to escort the victor off the battlefield, offer up some dubious virgin or other spoil as reward. Great accomplishment! The combat of non-entities. I embrace neither, no matter who triumphs. There is something that does not win or lose . . . I insist that my most powerful desire is to become sedulously indifferent to whatsoever happens to me.

Besides it is amusing that the two may be so artfully confused. To the vicious may I attribute an infallible divinity, while a devoted heart I permit only to attain to more vile humiliations. Do not mince at me 'the masochist really controls the sadist'. Both are under allegiance to a Master whose name is Limitation. Both delight in control and the break of control, and control again; the truth of prisons thrills victimizer and victim alike.

When I accepted as the order of things the rules of sadomasochism I designed for myself, whether I chose to be slave or master, a world where no power reigned but a capricious one, a random and human power that cares nothing, feels nothing for those who inhabit its kingdom. To exist in this grid expresses utter faithlessness in any order than that of a fanatic's whim. While sadomasochism enjoys all the forms of religious piety — kneeling, praying, worshipping, sacrificing, invoking and punishing — what fills the soul of the devotee is too often devoid of any idea of a greater destiny other than that of discovering the perfect Superior, or slave. That the Superior and the slave style themselves within their idealized roles, of worshipped and worshipper, punisher and punished and fix these boundaries irrevocably determines that, for all his bragged distinctiveness, the sadomasochist cannot sustain his illusion alone. His focus is always upon the Other.

Sadist and masochist believe that power is a matter of *temperament*. The sadist is born with it, rightfully wields it as is natural for the highly evolved being; while the masochist is naturally deficient, and furthermore so impaired as to be essentially incapable of garnering one particle of the dominating power. Those who are neither excessively cruel nor helpless are viewed as experiencing life by half-measure, inconsequentially, and with inane purpose. Such mediocrities do not understand what life is really all about . . . they have no all-engrossing possession — no slave — nor are they possessed entire — by a Superior . . .

As my conviction in my sadistic rights weakened, so grew my horror at the mildest example of the phenomenon. As I began to loathe my technical proficiency in violence, so more fervently did my slaves grovel. They agonized without my desire. It seemed my very cells were sadistic, I emanated dominion without willing. Futile to insist on my Superiority; to strike, shriek, contrive my power a superfluity. Less and less often did I drag out the complex and expensive apparatus of the domination 'trade'. And I realized, at last, that I was but a *witness* to the self-torment of the masochist, who required my condemning observance of their degradation — for a very special purpose. As one takes up a mirror to lend substance to oneself for a moment, so I lent the slave this mirror, bestowing upon the solitary masochist the vision of his worthlessness. Yet I was in the way; so guilt did not come to him from within, but from without, and now from a one revolted by her function, uneasy in her reign. "No! I'm not torturing myself, Mistress! It's you, *you're* doing it to me, *you're* making me suffer!"

I spent long hours with only my most devoted slaves, their ignoble lust simply satisfied by the command that they remain on their knees before me as I in turn stared into the mirror, trying in vain to see that other one again — to use her as I had before. Alas, or shall I say happily? she never once flickered into view. She was gone, and I felt burdened with the absolution of myself. I had to remain as one, one person, without her as my release. And how to resolve the pathetic, adoring one at my feet? Must I draw him into myself? I felt certain their abstract, desperate homage was not directed towards me, I was not worthy of it.

I stank to myself: I lost weight daily. Black felt most becoming, my nerves went exasperate under any other colour. The suspicion that I guarded a debilitating illness confirmed itself by the hour, through an arcana of symptoms... some illness of the womb. Finitude! my absolute, my dearest obsession, narrowed my brain to the work of dramatizing suicides. Each moment I was required to make a decision, to live up to an expectation, to maintain responsibility, I thought: Die, you convict! This difficulty I considered more than a few times a day: it came to be my sole possible response.

There were instants when what I recognized as clarity prevailed, when I recognized my decline as self-imposed. But the light was not continuous — what was revealed, for what purpose? — and between the steady self-torment and its one solution stood a strangely impassive panic. No school of knowledge or discipline could I stomach as authority, though I attempted to exploit some to divine the nature of my very grave curse. I fed this research through readings of the lives of great criminals; I defined myself within the accounts of the pathologies of famous psychotics. In short, I had conviction in nothing but my sickness to which I had so long ago been sentenced. I understood that my abandonment was imminent, already was my eye irretrievable, the hand excised from the heart. I came to depend totally upon my little slave . . . who in her deepest heart despises me. Yet I envy her. She claims she knows God, through her worship of me . . . but I knew that nothing would ever again possess for me the taint of the Essential.

How utterly like a masochist to consider more masochism — the constant attendance of adorers! — a cure! Perhaps you too believed in my programme, considered my 'achievements' to be true developments? I thought I had taken life so fiercely at the root, but persecutors unknown, you have waited, and rallied in far greater, insupportable numbers than I imagined you could . . . you ease into crevasses I never knew existed to flush me into the open. Long ago I created you, a minor detail, but it has come to pass that you are stronger than I!

My taste for humiliation scrounged up more fodder. I donned the sackcloth and ashes of the chronic sinner; I assumed an innate impotence. So fearful had I been of my victim-nature, yet it now seemed my one test was to embrace it. I had wandered at large long enough in this purulent waste, exiled from the Elect. But wasn't someone lying in wait for me, to kill me, once I did this . . . and I had lost the desire to defend myself . . .

"*. . . you will bend before the deity we choose, some bloodless (yet blood-stained) abstraction, our convenient dung-heap. Do penance in its name, intone the name over and over, please . . . Slough off your gross evil, peh! not so awful as you say, just a mistake . . . along with the millions of others we are in charge of, all as faceless, all as helpless, snarling like whelps in a den. We might revile you only for conceiving of an absolute Cruelty. There is no disorder of the angels! Are you not proud to snivel before us? We are watching, go on and lacerate yourself, that's what the nuns would have let you do, so long ago, get along now and despise yourself, ask God to forgive you, hope, trust, pray . . .*"

. . . what filthy behaviour!

"*. . . you will be your own victim now, you will do with yourself as you* *will. Leave off this stiff obscurity of the Superior . . . there is no correct sadist . . .*"

All defences deranged, death imminent — that, or love. From the most intimate friend to the stranger I attend the violent blow. Who now is the true carrier of brutality? My life is willing to be discarded, if only the potential vandal would give notice! I am pawing my ground, I will end my vagaries, but how can I take the bit in my own teeth?

Unabated the schizosomata, for another I am creating memories, for myself I spiral out in too frail an extension. The coat upon the floor — is that my crumpled body? This piece of furniture might topple over and crush me, soundlessly. All the blood out of me drains, the black dress, no, the black dress drains . . . so white flies my skin, everything so murderously black white BLACK. This furtive disgust for her curdles and hardens into sombre clouds.

One evening a Mistress of my acquaintance stopped by my torture-chamber to gossip. She regaled me with a fantastic horror-story, one that in a sudden consciousness of the sinister end of my work inspired such revulsion, a familiar feverishness... I had thought myself unable any longer to be shocked, but I was so by her tale — though a hysterical noise like a laugh welled to my lips at the pathetic ironies of the sadomasochist. So follows her account of 'The Cannibal Society'.

"There exists an elite of masochistic men, who have gone so far as to find pleasure in revealing to one another their depraved lusts (unlike most who stay isolated in their shame). They engage in competitions to outdo one another in the indulgence of utter abjectness. Their sensibilities have so developed, or degenerated in concert, that only the most reprobate women can satisfy them. It must be very difficult for them to procure these women, and keep their service on tap; that their existence has been made known to me is very fortunate for us. I can make you an offer, and a very generous one, if you are interested. You ask, what is required of you?

"These five 'exalted' masochists enjoy their humiliation in

many ways, yet all variations culminate in one mode, and one only, which for them is the epitome of all: they require that they be devoured — literally. The female sadist plays the part of a ravenous vampire, who enters the bed-chamber of each gentleman during the night, and must not only bite their throats and drain off the blood issuing therefrom, but is enjoined to rip off pieces of the flesh, chew, and swallow the disgusting gobbets. One of the company, who I presume acted as initiator of the others, has indulged himself for so long his torso is quite detestably scarred. In the morning, you can imagine their comparisons at the breakfast table, the reflections upon their gouges, upon the variations of method: avidity of bite, length of attack, and so on . . .

"The few women who permit them to glut their inverted cannibalism have had their teeth filed to an edge that makes precise the rending of flesh . . . though the five are always on the lookout for a young sadist to introduce into their foul rite. For they say there is nothing to compare with the hesitant, then frenzied passion of naturally sharp teeth gnawing into the epidermis. They describe, with a connoisseur's delicate gestures and little sighs, the breathless instant before the female actually pierces the skin; the sudden tremor of her disgust, how the bite relaxes as the conscience revives — oh will she go on? — and when she does, and the bite is accomplished and the blood rushes into the mouth, they speak of the ecstatic consummation of power with powerlessness, as the victim knows himself drunk of his life's fluid."

. . . he embraces his Death, and She bites into the wound that has been open so long it has gone black . . . she widens it, makes a cavity, a pit of what was the soul, rummages deep into the vitals and at last consumes the heart. Then, lacking in nothing, does he realize orgasm — having ceased to exist.

That very evening a victim was presented to me who desired I use razors upon his body any way I desired, but he had to be tied to the crucifix throughout. I agreed, for my curiosity along with my disgust had been sparked by my friend's story. I wished to know if I was capable of drawing blood. It was a point of honour for me to investigate this facet of my sadism.

Once stretched on the crucifix, the slave submitted to having his genitals tightly bound with thin leather cords that had been soaked in salted water. Once my assistant had prepared him, I strolled in and furiously sliced into the bulging flesh which instantly grew turgid. Drops of blood glittered from the shallow slash. I continued making cuts, intent on designing a pattern, but the sight of a small red puddle at his feet frightened me and I abruptly exited. As I fumbled in a closet for disinfectant, bandages, I felt queerly light, gay and empty-headed in contrast to my act.

I then prevented myself from going to his aid — it was not in character for me to help him. He ought to be left to bleed, I recalled, and touched up my lipstick. In confused array ran the memory of Christ in the Garden of Gethsemane, sweating blood in his agony, calling upon his Father to take the cup from him. He knew he was to undergo intense torture the following day. Why did he ask God to revoke his trial? Did he think the pain would be too much, was he frightened? Did he at last rawly recognize, and abhor the conditions of human existence? I considered for the thousandth time my own crucifixion. But I welcomed the cup, I relished my suffering, I wanted to die . . .

I returned to my victim and roughly staunched the blood with a towel. I showed anger with his ruining the carpet, but he sensed my trembling and whimpered, "Please Mistress, don't be nice to me, let me bleed for you." I had heard such lines before — this creature was perfectly sincere. So I followed his reasoning and slapped him repeatedly cross the face, and as he sagged on the cross stiffly replied, "I've had enough of you for tonight, you're going home early, you little bore," and loosened his bonds myself.

I quit the chamber. An arctic air flailed my legs, swirled the day's debris into wild eddies. I stood on the corner for a cab. Two dark-skinned women loped by at high speed, tailed perfunctorily by a squad-car. The officers looked through me. Passers-by cowered against the fierce and random lunging of the frozen wind, but I felt revitalized by the relentless attack. With a familiar longing I gazed up into the aery reaches of the skyscrapers, whose cables and antennae tore at the clouds under the unrelieved buffets of winter's full force. How pleasant to be up there, I mooned, in a perfect tempest! But when a cab pulled up I ducked into its heated belly and named another destination.

After that first time it was not at all difficult for me to cut him. I amused myself drawing patterns on his thighs, breaking into old wounds so each time he left the mark was deeper, and took longer to heal. I invented other pleasures — such as refusing to take out the blade at all, aggravating his servility ten-fold. I forced him to slash at himself to entertain me; as well, he delighted in being robbed once in bondage. But as I thrust my hand into his trouser-pocket one evening I felt a sharp pain. The clever monster had devised an unwrapped razor-blade in place of the usual wad of cash to greet my hand. I said nothing, and I am sure he revelled in my pain. Though he called for several months afterwards I refused to see him. He visited with my associates, "But they don't know how to hurt me like you do," he whined on the phone. In time I was able to repel him . . .

Marking from that evening my blood was shed in turn I began to draw back from the Superior. Though for a long period I had abhorred her, it was not 'til I knew a revenge for my gloating, useless blood-shedding that my soul decisively recoiled. Through the extraction of a victim's life-fluid I had gained admittance into a new order — from whose logic I had to retreat, lest through my waxing attraction to blood I commit a murder. But I wonder if I could not simply name it 'sacrifice', and proceed with my victim's destruction calmly, naturally — and with his full consent?

A stagnant void, where I ask again and again: who is the vampire, and who the drained. The question of control has fled, superficial: death controls all. The plump and hopeful victim — sadist, masochist — embraces the vortex that like a disembodied mouth eats without satiation.

Again, consider suicide: after which, that blurred utopia 'heaven' or some ghost's-walk attends. I hope there is nothing, there — what peace then. The seductive vagueness of the prospect segues nicely with my present languor. To avoid dying, though, perhaps I should teach myself faith in a greater purpose, yes that would be nice! but I suppose I will have to invent it — I cannot stomach anything ready-made. That way, I could revive myself under the conviction that my crimes and suffering are all part of a larger Plan. Certainly I would like to believe that my pain is orderly.

I choose not to kill myself, I want to keep my bad faith, I want to go on indulging my righteous violence against those who welcome it. But I have elicited the choice, I cannot avoid it now. So I fade back into my hesitation, drowsily toss the 'reasons' around, fall asleep, letting the last considered lend itself to my vacancy for a couple of days. But it does happen, on occasion, that I am galvanized to take myself in hand, at the idea of my crude, untimely death by some random force . . .

Very well . . . assume a purpose for your trial. Force yourself! to trust that this purpose exists, though it is unknown to you, so that the attendant suffering will not debilitate you. Let the very existence of it goad you, spark the absurd within you so you have permission to go violent, to go on violent, still alert to some 'will of the greater'. Suicidal you are lacking in imagination, dream now of this greater destiny for yourself!

But this is where I started . . .

Within the narrow walls where the sadist's ephemeral caress is granted the masochist blossoms, and the hideous being, that exaggerate vice preens herself, tramples herself, shrieks siren-like when the victim twitches of his own free will . . . he perfumes the air with a rubbery stink . . . there is no escaping this room, where the sadist is host to the grateful parasite. Oh, why the histrionics?

. . . for I have created a world in my own image, a pretty tale of laceration, designed by the face that spits in its face. Within this room there is no success, only failure to drain, failure to submit and the repeated attempts. Inane as this struggle is I keep on with it. My will to destroy itself, stopping short of the final cut, must soon pall! I will excoriate my heart, 'til feeling ends, and I cry at last . . . that I cannot feel.

We hear that strife naturally resolves into victory. But I exhume one excuse, then another, to irritate the enemy, bring him forth. I must drain life away into Nothing, slowly and steadily, 'til in that grandeur I may reign: the annihilatory grandeur of the second death. I wish there to be no hope for me, no hope at all. In the grip of this idea, death and the sense of a greater purpose become one and the same.

I and my slavish cohorts continue to suffer and create more suffering. This is our pastime, it makes us feel alive. Our lust, by which we distinguish ourselves, is the lust for death whom we worship. Morbidly do we cultivate this instinct for what extinguishes itself. I need not improve myself — I am perfect. Superfluous and senseless restriction, 'improvement'. I need only maintain a stableful of passive men I may vampirize as I require. They in turn are eager to be drained. What difference can it make? my pleasure is my purpose, death the end of it all, inevitable, she shuffles in quiet like the clean-up woman, quick, efficient, to the secret relief of the host of the dirty revelry . . .

Here follows a dream; a visit; and a dream. That I did cease my sadistic practices is a fact. How I did it I may explore endlessly but I cannot explain. I had a dream, I visited a friend, I dreamed again — and I stopped. Why this sequence decided me I am not sure. But I am glad to give no rational excuse for my obsession's death — if she is dead.

I dreamed I was in Paris: I stood in a street in a panic need to take a test, the nature of which was exceedingly important, as it would reunite me with the one I loved. That I might not arrive at the testing-place by four o'clock had me dashing through alleys and byways, quite at random and without heeding obstacles in my path. I came to a railway station, where a great mass of humanity thronged, all as desperate as I to be somewhere other than where we were. With frantic gestures I applied to a monumental desk whose top surface I could barely reach, behind which stood a row of tall, imperious women wearing an official uniform. They resolutely ignored me and my inquiries, involved as they were in apparently petty duties of an arcane significance, which they performed as tricks of sleight-of-hand, with obscure but authoritative aplomb. At last I achieved the attention of one, though she leaned forward but slightly to hear me. To my alarm I had become incoherent in French. As I stuttered and made idiocy of my simple request, she gazed down at me with a serious, bland face. I returned this gaze with some difficulty, as I was blinded by the milky white brilliance of a light diffused by the opaque panes of the iron-cage roof. At last, through an extreme force of the will on my part, was I able to make my intent known. She handed me an enormous sheaf of papers and directed me out of the station. At that I knew I had made the right connection.

Now all I needed to do was read the instructions on the first sheet, and I would discover where I had to go to take the test, which I held in my hand. As I whiled my way out of the station, and turned down a long incline towards the river, I riffled through the thick manuscript. Once more did I writhe in despair, for not only had my speaking French degenerated, but neither could I decipher the written word. This peculiar inability irritated me to the ends of every nerve in my body, and I stopped dead on the incline. Had some profound change been made in the language, that my knowledge was rendered obsolete? How had this occurred without my slightest awareness? I struggled with the manuscript, squinting at it and turning it round every which way. I knew if I couldn't break into it, I would miss the test and never again see the one I loved. It was approaching four o'clock.

I went slowly down the incline, my eyes fixed on the manuscript. When I reached the riverbank, the words snapped to focus with a piercing clarity. Never had I read French so avidly before, with such comprehension, and I absorbed the information I required and read on and on distractedly into the manuscript. But then I forced myself to attend to the place of testing, as the bell-tower sounded out the fourth hour. It was in the great cathedral of Notre-Dame, just behind me . . .

I turned, in the happy conviction I would arrive in good time. Yet all my strength proved not enough to take me up the incline. No sooner did I put one foot down, than the one behind refused to budge. When I painfully dragged it up to meet the other, my knees so buckled and I was so unnerved I had to rest before attempting again. I forged on, to where the edifice seemed to hover in air, ominous and dark. No light showed in the spiralling rose-window, and in the sudden dimness of the day so few details could I discern in all the carved stone of the mass it resembled a distant, pinnacled mountain. I managed to make a little trembling progress, only to have the ground surge up, and distend . . . so was my passage to the place of testing actively obstructed.

I woke up in a rage, legs rigid from straining to climb . . . I knew something very serious was at hand, and I resolved to speak to an old friend who had long ago rejected me when I took up my sadistic interests.

"How good to see you, after so long a time," he greeted me politely. I knew behind the careful cordiality was contempt ready to spring. "It's curious you should call, I was just thinking of you. I have something to show you that's very much to your taste," and he beckoned me into his study.

From a box of worn brown leather he withdrew a packet of what appeared to be banknotes. "These are from the fifteenth century," and he handed them to me. "It was thought paper-money was not printed then, but my dealer has assured me these franc-notes are from the year 1452, used only by the king and his court in their transactions — in gambling, most likely." The bills were as small as playing-cards, and so intricately drawn and coloured the literal figuration of the design was near indistinguishable. I examined all of them, their different denominations and patterns; altogether I estimated their value at one hundred seventy-three thousand dollars. "Why aren't these in a museum?" I accused him, "You must have paid a fortune for them." "It was my fortune," he replied, "to pay almost nothing for them, and they will surely make my fortune one day." A sudden, harsh sadness came over me.

"They are fakes," I pronounced, "You have been cheated." He covered the box with one hand, slid it into a drawer and shut it. "So your aesthetic sense has deserted you, too," he said softly, "something that was once your greatest virtue. Still, is it not an elementary truth," and he spoke with a rising passion, though without anger, "that some objects are so rare, so beautiful in themselves, what hard cash they might be converted into is valueless next to their true worth." I responded callously, "So you paid hard cash for them. Was it a good investment, or not?" "I am not interested in reducing them to a commodity, why would I want to liquidate their authority over my senses? If I chose to do so, I would lose much more than money, my friend," and he enveloped my whole person in one long serious gaze.

I renewed the quarrel. "So granting your lovely possession is a kind of forgery, still you don't care, claiming the value placed upon an object is a decision made essentially by the imagination." "Yes — and as much as they were valued at the instant of their conception, within the creator's mind, I say that spiritual value remains imbedded within it forever and sets the true price." "True price, true worth," I muttered, "what lies! You make it all up." I recalled myself, from his silence, to a more courteous demeanour, and resumed, "I have a problem with this. In the translation of this impalpable, spiritual worth into the realm of dollars and cents, a mistake could be made." "Yes, certainly, and by necessity. For within this interim the subtle increment known as the moral value is imposed, and as one is a guardian of virtue, or a model of viciousness . . ." here a certain archness invaded his tone . . . "the former will join the original intention with a corresponding high or low price, while the latter will divert this intention into association with a false price."

I felt myself quickening under the influence of his clarity. "So a price, high or low, signifies nothing of the value of a thing . . . nothing but whether a sublime or a degraded imagination set it." "Precisely. It is the assets of the imagination that raise and lower the value of an object accordingly, as one is rich or impoverished within. So that for the one who ill-conceives value, things in themselves ineffably precious may be valued at nothing, while grossness and triviality will come high-priced, though in time I believe a true angelic motive overcomes any degradation."

With a failing sarcasm I asked him, "So how do you resolve such incongruity? What measures have you invented, what standards have you immovably set?" "I cannot answer you easily. Each day do I adjust my judgement..." "So you admit the standards change continually..." "Not at all — but each day my perception of motives, exalted or debased may alter, as I train myself to be more sharply attuned to the truth, which sets the course of my judgements." I fell silent; then, trusting him, I faltered, "Once I believed in the existence of this truth... I have experienced it, or I believed I did. To realize it again..." but all at once I could not go on, I found myself so agitated. My friend spoke not a word, it was as though I were alone in the room, speaking to myself. Yet I knew he listened, and I whispered, "So you think there may really be such a thing as evil, and the good, with no confusion, no possible blur between them..." "...without a subsequent humiliation of the beautiful, and glorification of the loathesome." Thus did he well-complete my sentence.

I do not believe I paid my host a very fair good-evening, for I scarce recall leaving his apartment. But that was so like me. Had he cursed me and driven me from the room, would I not have clung to him, and snarled back, and begged him to please return my call soon?

I passed that evening in a torpor, and each second trailed by with the irrevocable challenge — to act, and act now. Yet was I so oppressed it seemed I would sooner die than move from my chair to bed. What was the exact nature of this excruciant urgency? I could think only in terms of the unfinished dream. I knew I had to arrive at the cathedral or mountain and so just before abandoning consciousness that evening I recollected the scene and its mood, gave myself up to sleep with the intent to reach the 'place of testing' and undergo the trial.

My sleep was immediate and profound, and the dream emerged as follows: I stood within an enormous vault, as belittling as the vast enclosed space of a cathedral, but a broad staircase in its centre led up to an open second-storey gallery. I took this stair in the company of someone, invisible but audible. A great throng sedately took their exercise there, circling round and round in silent pleasure. Above the crowd the stone arc'd unimpeded, to distant points, one which broke the stone and through whose circular vent light filtered down throughout the great concavity, infusing all faces with a clear pale radiance.

Branching off from this grand promenade were rooms that my

mysterious interlocutor made me a tour of. They numbered twenty-two, and I remarked to him on the significance of this number. But he made no reply.

Again we passed through the twenty-two chambers, and this time more slowly. Among the inhabitants of each I searched for the one I loved. One of the rooms was extremely plain and furnished with low, flat beds. Sitting upright and stony-faced on these pallets was a group of little orphans, who gazed at me with hostile surprise. Many of the other rooms were crowded and close and filled me with loathing. It was with some pleasure that I was led to my own room, wherein, I was told, I might wait for the one I loved.

My room was suffocatingly luxurious, and I wondered at this compared to the others' spareness. The impression of dirt and confusion outside my room thrust me deeply into its heart, and I roamed its four corners with a sense of safety inviolate. Three large windows looked over a rather homely, but cheerful garden that was familiar to me. But my bed impressed me more than anything.

The massive wooden frame was carved as though it were a piece of church-furniture, ornate, deeply crevassed, with figures, it seemed, frozen in allegory. But when I focused upon its design I could not make out any details. I attempted over and over, but at last lapsed into a sort of wonderment at how the carvings blurred and drew away the more intently I gazed. I relinquished the pursuit, then, satisfied by the appearance of richness and fine workmanship. The bed was so broad and slippery I could barely climb up, but I precariously settled at last in its centre.

The lines of a golden lamp by the bed, worked in a lily-shape, also eluded my gaze. At angles to the foot of my bed were two other beds, both small and narrow. Happily only one was occupied, by a frail and sickly creature named Virginia. She spoke to me in a faint voice, but I scarcely showed the commonest courtesy in appearing to listen. A full hush fell, in that I sat idly waiting.

I gazed about me, and I saw not far beyond me, content with

the vague luxury I found precisely correspondent with myself and mine. Everything is perfectly harmonious, I intoned. As I sat the light grew faint, and I noticed candles burning all about the room. The girl Virginia disappeared so that I sat alone in the gathering darkness. Quieter waned the room as if the air were being drawn out, though the candle-flames leapt high and refulgent. Under their palpitate light the exact nature of the room clarified itself, as though a focusing lens slowly rotated into place cross my eyes.

The carvings on the bed sprang to life in obscene array, of snakes and goats in mortal combat, of bloated hideous flowers twisting round sleeping figures in sexual embrace, whose eyes but partly open already revealed their disgust. My golden lamp was a monstrous fungus, glowing with an ochre phosphorescence. Veils that had drifted so pleasingly in the tepid breeze, with such gossamer effect were revealed as metal mesh, filth-caked and rent where something had struggled in its net without success. The crude accoutrements of black-magic rites, rags, tattered manuscripts, bowls where rose the faint residue of a rank perfume, wavy-bladed knives and interminable lengths of rope strewed the floor. Sensuously, achingly, a kind of ooze effect magnified the loathesome atmosphere; one by one the objects came to press their mucous soul upon me; then, as though performing, the entire room shimmered in its rich and consoling glamour, before swerving back in light dance-step from falsity to pierce with the wretched truth.

I glided off the bed and went to the corner of the room, to a door set exactly in the corner, in the V of the two walls. As I stood there the door swung open and once more was the simple and unaffected glory of the garden shown me. I wanted very much to walk there but I could not, I was only allowed to look, as between my door and the ground there was no stair. For a long time I surveyed the majestic trees, lush beds of yellow blossoms, the grassy walks; then turned away in resigned melancholy.

"So why didn't you jump?" ". . . the thought did not occur to me . . ."

The room quickly filled with the darting, insignificant figures of the orphans. The furnishings had further deteriorated to a desolate cheapness, and a squalid coloration overpowered the room, a miasma of brownish-grey. All the windows were bricked over, and I sensed the room as far underground. The false one I loved arrived, the one who I knew was diverting me from the true one. We were informed that we were students, and still had hours of lessons to do. We were not permitted to sleep . . . we had to write essays. Yet despite my seemingly degraded status, sparks of energy convulsed my limbs, and I realized my work was directive of the entire under-story of the cathedral of Notre Dame . . .

I went back to my source, to trace the origin of my incitement to practise sadism. I sought the phrase that would encapsule the charm of my former delusion, the paragraph whose central lie had seduced me into the tedious and degrading compulsion. Where was the noxiously perfumed passage that had first enthralled me? Behind every pronouncement, lewd or philosophical, flashed the Marquis' obese posturing figure, impotent and red in the face from a tantrum . . . forever helpless in a lunatic asylum. Such a model . . . !

One part of his faculties had operated intact, and to excess — an imagination that elaborated upon his lust for revenge. He wished to forever humiliate the woman who had placed him in confinement for the rest of his life. Exciting himself endlessly upon images of torturing and abusing 'virtue', he had given her hundreds of faces, had drawn upon these lascivious, energizing visions as the sole sustenance of his impoverished existence. He was never to realize these fantasies upon her person — but he wrote them all out. Their extreme virulence survives to this day, their unexorcised power put rigorously into practice by a cult of devotees . . . the masturbatory dreams of a psychopath?

At last I found something that tinged me with my former arousal. I tried to feel humiliated that such sophistry had incited me to crime; still, I can not solve the problem this passage provokes and so fluently resolves:

> *We will pass for an instant into Nature's crucible thence to spring up again under other shapes, and that, without there being any more prerogatives for him who madly smoked up Virtue's effigy than for the other who wallowed in all the most disgraceful excesses, because there is nothing by which Nature is offended and because all men, equally her womb's issue, during their term having acted not at all save in accordance with her impulsions, will all of them meet with after their existence, both the same end and the same fate.*

If to do evil, or good, garners one the same reward — death, and the worms; if to perpetrate the cruellest act, or to assuage it is all the same to Nature, dull goddess; does not the distinction between good and evil lose its edge, and the choice between pain and pleasure prevail?

My violence acts in one as an inspiration to studiously avoid my example; in another I provoke imitation — both, for their pleasure. To balance my viciousness, must there not be a corresponding and equal specimen of holiness? Do I not thwart the appearance of a still more sublime soul if I fail to realize my degeneracy to the maximum?

. . . No, you will not countenance yourself as an author of evil any longer. You must revolt against the idea of your immortal soul being consumed like some common shred, in an impersonal fire, in an explosion of darkness. Give yourself your true value. Swallow the bloody clot of vengeance against the one who had imprisoned you for the rest of your life. Forgive him, and yourself. Resolve against expressing too well your sadism, in thought, word, deed . . . Restrain it, so it

by degrees becomes passive, 'til it is only the shadow of desire . . .

Do all this in remembrance of me.

You, the sadist, are charged with the control of the masochist. Take heed of her, and no one else. You are not permitted contact with anyone else. You may not speak to them, you are too full of hatred. As well, you may not pose as myself, for I at present am but a starved little embryo and must be left to myself to recover.

Prevent her from running too heedlessly into the fray, without a backward glance, as she so loves to do. Devoted to you who are an illusion, she gladly destroys herself to approach you. But yesterday she asked me for release from you, which surprised me. Her trial beneath you has been long, but I cannot grant this release to her yet. For you surely need her, and I too require her presence... lest you attack me. Besides, if I killed her now, she could simply revive herself and smile at me! She is numb, very numb, to the core — sometimes she appears to have fallen into an imponderable sleep yet beneath your hand she rejoices. She is resting on the sill of a precipice, where we may not follow... see, her eyes are clear and overflowing.

... Resolved at last to my position, I am reunited with the one I love and we return to the mansion that is our true home. Our hands are so entwined there is no distinction between my hand and hers. Together we climb the great staircase, and take our place among those who stroll the round. Later we will enter our inviolate room, where the Master of the house and his Lady will come to kiss us goodnight. My duties in regard to her have been thoroughly explained to me, where we may walk, and where we ought to run. At last has she been returned to me, and I have not left her side for an instant. She is not well . . .

All is in order within this house. Even the wretched being whom I love (strange spawn for so noble a pair!) is strong and passionate. Though born into the greatest wealth, she is unconscious of it. She cannot take the gold into her own hand, yet she plays all day with her mother's jewels. I must watch her to see she does not swallow them, so fond is she of putting them into her mouth.

The stories I tell her are very special, no other child in the house is allowed to hear them. I myself am not even permitted to gaze for long upon the other children, they say my methods brutalize the ordinary child. I am too subtle and strange . . . yet for the one I love best, my ardour just barely keeps pace with her intense hunger for my eyes and embrace.

Once she escaped me, and it was then I recognized my grave responsibility. She raged . . . she tore at the ladies' gowns, threatened the men with her pocket-knife and almost strangled a little girl. She rampaged through the kitchen, spilling the milk and extinguishing the fire. She provoked her mother's tears and the guards' hilarity. I captured her, tied her up tightly and left her in a closet for a day. Still, so savage a mood had taken possession of her that when I restored her limbs to her and confidently began a story, she leaped at my face and tore at my eyes.

You will not see me often outside our chamber. You will catch no glimpse of me out of doors, enjoying the garden in the company of a gentleman. You will miss me among the others taking their meal and laughing aloud. These are not my allotments; I tread there at our peril. It demands all my energy, every second of my waking concentration to watch over my charge, to ensure the quiet passing of each day in this great house.

Flawed, the body convulsed beneath an invisible hand. Masturbatory, same story, of twisted impossible limbs in sheets. The blade of the guillotine's raised so she will below, as sepulchral work, carefully carve round the fault.

Faultless, distinct, her breakage's invoked; so ends the voluptuous veer to the edge. All past is controlled, and panic submissive — it was an interesting experiment. An involution, a drain-off, a desolation by necessity. Came the final dissection: the corpse was too torn to decipher. Splayed, cut, chewed to a shred it was at last a success and passed on. Done, the stinking finale, the breathless last turn, I was close entombed, stitched up as carrion for vultures attendant. Yet the service has only now begun — and what's left might go white, might not.

OTHER BOOKS BY BLUE MOON AUTHORS

Anonymous
Souvenirs from a Boarding School

Edith Cadivec
Eros: The Meaning of My Life

David (Sunset) Carson
Lament

Gerald and Caroline Greene
S-M: The Last Taboo

Denise Hall
A Brief Education

Jac Lenders
Excess of Love

Richard Manton
Max

Alexander Trocchi
Helen and Desire